CORPORATE DEFIANCE

NICOLE

SIR MARK ANTHONY

ISBN
978-1-963254-32-7 (Paperback)
978-1-963254-33-4 (eBook)

Corporate Defiance

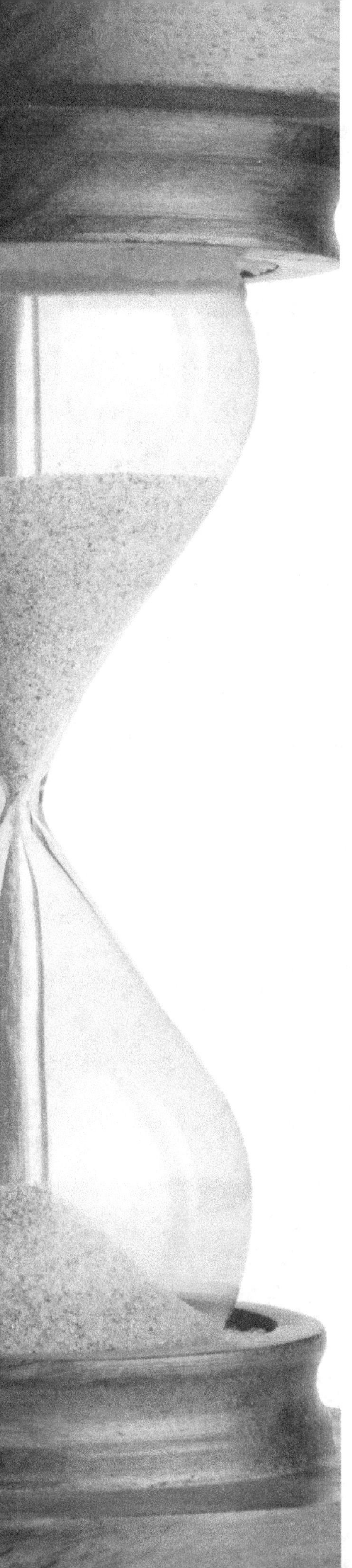

Table of Contents

The majority of the board knew that Nicole Gershom was the one they wanted after they interviewed her for the third time to become its Chairman and Chief Executive Officer of Maywell Electronics. Even though some board members balked at the idea at first because they considered it treason in letting an outsider come in to run the company. They could not deny that Nicole was the right person for the job. Plus, women in general have become powerful business moguls in the business world. Plus, Nicole had exceptional skills along with an impressive background to run a major conglomerate, like Maywell. Nicole's hiring brought about big changes at the computer giant. When word first got out that Maywell hired a woman to head the company, women activist groups around the country applauded Maywell's decision, not to mention the company shares rose thirty-three percent on the New York Stock Exchange. Board members thought this was a sign of good things to come, at least they hoped so. The company needed some good news for a change after a major shake-up like this. However, for the moment things were finally looking up. Maywell had been without a permanent CEO for several months as some board members took on or shared some of the company's major responsibilities, but John Aslong was the interim CEO during this time.

The No. 1 job had become vacant when former CEO, Ty Dannerman II resigned under some unusual circumstances, which Maywell wanted to keep quiet about.

Dannerman, a computer expert received the bad news via e-mail. Maywell was very evasive about company business and imposed a gag order on all company employees that nothing should be leaked to the press concerning this matter. Mr. Dannerman was reassigned to the board of directors at the company as a peace offering. Company board members are as follows:

- Paul Monday,
  President, East Lang Corporation

- Willard Trust,
  Retired CEO, Lee Pharmaceutical

- J.J Anton, Jr.,
  Dean of New York University
  School of Accounting

- Robert Lowe,
  CEO, Journal Bank & Trust

- John Aslong,
  Executive Vice President
  Maywell Electronics

- Edward Seator,
  President of Corporate Affairs
  Maywell Electronics

- Harold Comet,
  CEO, Thompson Corporation

- Shelby McFord,
  CEO, Island Bank & Trust

- Sid McBream,
  COO, Maywell Electronics

- Austin Gallop,
  CEO, LTT Corporation

- Alvin Stillwell,
  President of Marketing
  Maywell Electronics

- Ty G. Dannerman II.
  Former CEO, Maywell Electronics

The board found nothing that they disliked about Nicole. They voted 10 to 1 in favor of Nicole's hiring with one abstaining. Mr. Dannerman voted against while Mr. Gallop abstained. Board members examined Nicole's resume for the umpteenth time, they ran background check after background check. They dissected her life from the conception of her mother's womb until the very day they hired her. They knew every little thing about her, from her blood type to her favorite dish. They knew all about Nicole's past. They found no blemishes on her record, nothing that would come back and haunt them or stir up controversy down the road. Nicole's credentials were superb. She was damn near perfect which board members thought was highly unusual because everybody has some skeletons in their closet. Hell, they dissected her life as though they were looking for some reason to not to hire her.

Nicole was an exceptional student, valedictorian in every school she graduated from, including head start until she received her doctorate degree at the tender age of twenty-two. Her parents raised her to be proper. Her credentials were impeccable, a true professional in every sense of the word with a proven track record. Nicole was a widow with no kids, the one thing that eluded her in her life. Her husband, Robert was killed in the Vietnam War and she almost had a nervous breakdown, overcoming bouts with depression, which the board members overlooked because it showed a true test of Nicole's character, a real trooper. Nicole knew her newfound responsibilities would keep her married to the company. She knew this was the type of job that generated power and wealth. A job that could make you lose, your soul if you are not careful, but she welcomed the challenge.

Maywell was the innovator in the computer industry. They were head and shoulders above the rest, a trendsetter. Maywell wanted desperately to change its image and the way the public perceived the company. This was because the EEOC and the Federal Judicial System had come down hard on some of the industry computer giants and almost put them out of business. There were lawsuits filed everywhere trying to break-up companies to force them into submission. Some thought the government was sending corporate America a strong message by making examples out of these companies. Maywell wanted a more conservative image. An image not made up of a bunch of stiff-neck white-collar executives whose main concern is making money. But a company that hire minorities that cares about the environment, educational issues, and giving money to charities.

It was a no brainer in hiring Nicole because she was sensitive to all the issues Maywell distanced itself from, but felt they were important. She looked good on paper and was very impressive on her three interviews. She came in with a business plan, a plan as easy as one, two, three on how to generate business, which was very detailed oriented. She was their top choice. In fact, board members called off the search for other candidates. The list was a very short one to say the least.

The board members appointed John Aslong to spearhead the search and he convinced the board that Nicole was the one they were looking for. Mr. Aslong, a fifty-seven-year-old, had been with Maywell since his college years as an intern. Mr. Aslong always knew he wanted to work for Maywell at a tender young age when he was growing up in the southeast. His godfather, Eddie Banks, whom he loved dearly, was a top executive with Maywell before he died of lung cancer when John was only fourteen years old. He sold John on the idea of becoming a businessman, especially with Maywell because they took care of their employees. Maywell had been in operation since 1895 and was founded by Francis Maywell, who had a vision to create a world wide vision through electronics. Mr. Banks made a hell of an impression on John. John admired Mr. Banks expensive suits and use to play dress-up in front of the mirror each morning before he went to school. Mr. Banks instilled in John that you can be anything you want to be and at the time of Mr. Banks death, young John vowed he would one-day work for Maywell and become his godfather's direct reflection.

....

As the Gershom era begins, Ty Dannerman is already the forgotten man, the odd man out mainly because Maywell was looking to move forward. A man driven by power and demanded it. He had Maywell employees walking on eggshells during his rein as CEO.

Dannerman told Maywell investors, shareholders, and board members that he would work with Nicole even though he voted against her hiring. Board members hoped this was the case because they didn't need a Judas Iscariot to wreck havoc on the company. They thought this act was revolutionary especially coming from a man as power driven as Dannerman. A position such as this demand power and respect because people revere and extol you. Dannerman had done some wonderful things for Maywell during his tenure, but the nature of the business is not what you have done in the past, but what have you done for me lately.

Dannerman's declaration that he would work together with Nicole was seen as modest, given the circumstances surrounding his resignation. He was known for his hard line approach. Some called it heartless others called it imposing, but Dannerman called it respect. He demanded respect. He revered his position as to being a prime minister, the go to guy, and he demanded respect from every employee at Maywell, from the boiler room to the boardroom. He was an innovator and to compare him to any other CEO would have been unfair because being the CEO at Maywell was just a step beneath being President of the United States. The job executed that much power and influence.

As quiet as it was kept, everyone at Maywell was pleased that Dannerman had been ousted as CEO, but was more pleased that Dannerman would remain loyal to the company. His declaration shined the light on a dark situation and removed any doubt of him abandoning the ship. It removes the threat of lawsuits that could have been tied up in court for years. It also removed the threat of having to deal with negative publicity, behind the scene wrangling and backbiting, pitting one side against the other. Dannerman went as far as saying that he would make a public statement concerning his resignation. Board members balked at this idea because they wanted the dust to settle. This was a smoking gun and after the smoke cleared they wanted Nicole to be the only one standing in the forefront.

Dannerman had an uncanny relationship with the board members because he shot straight from the hip. Whatever came up came out of his mouth. He meant what he said and said what he meant. The truth of the matter is that he thought he was more powerful than the board, which he overshadowed. He was the computer expert that pulled himself up by his own bootstraps. Coming from a humble beginning and winding up as one of the world's richest and powerful men. He let it be known he was the one running Maywell, the man right here. Recently he was running the company right into the ground with his latest antics and wheeling and dealings. He was out of control and when board members reached out to him, he was unapproachable not to mention arrogant.

Never before had Maywell had a CEO so daunting that it threatened to create problems for the company. Dannerman didn't trust anyone. He kept his friends close and his enemies even closer. The joke around the company was that he was the invisible CEO. He only made public appearances when it was absolutely necessary other than that you hardly ever saw him. In meetings when he wasn't absent or late, he was constantly differential to the board. He asked the questions, made the decisions and commanded attention. When he talked he demanded everyone to listen, he was the big cheese.

When Dannerman was named CEO of Maywell it wasn't by circumstance. It was a careful drawn out plan. He campaigned for the position. It was not what he knew, it was who, he knew. He had the support of some of the influential people at the company. He majored in computer science in college and went to work for Maywell as an intern through the college job placement office. He worked his way up through the ranks by undermining some key people at the company by becoming a yes man. He let it be known what his intentions were, becoming CEO at Maywell one day. He was very ambitious as he was coming up through the ranks at Maywell. Through this attempt he formed some strong allies and finally ended up as Maywell's CEO. He invested his money well in stocks and bonds through the years. This act alone gained him some brownie points with some of the head honchos at the company, most people would have been content with building their portfolio, but not Dannerman, he wanted it all. His motto was give him the power and the money would come.

When Dannerman became CEO at Maywell he told the board that he simply wanted to be a team player, a true professional that worked for the good of the company. He wanted the company to succeed with his innovative ideas and that he would pull no punches. The board felt Dannerman was a man of his word and wanted him to succeed. Heck, they gave him every opportunity to succeed. Everything was at his disposal. They had hoped that he would mature, that he had been spanked, put to bed and woke up all grown up, so much so that he would grow with the company. It was all good at first. He arrived at his office around 8:00 a.m. each morning and his secretary would brief him on his agenda for that day. The role of CEO at Maywell was to put the company first and board members really thought Dannerman would set a high precedent, a new mark, one that would carry the company into the next millennium. They were confident that he would. When he vowed that he would work with Nicole for the good of the company, they viewed him in a different light.

CHAPTER
2

Old man Maywell built Maywell's reputation upon image. Image was not everything it was the only thing. It was Maywell's creed that all company employees honor this creed with the up most integrity. Ty Dannerman, a high roller with a bad boy image was simply running on borrowed time. Company investors and shareholders had grown tired of Mr. Dannerman's latest tactics and antics. They felt that Mr. Dannerman was leading Maywell down the wrong path that could eventually bankrupt the company. Mr. Dannerman informed company investors and shareholders at their annual shareholders meeting in San Jose, California that he made mistakes by trying to expand Maywell into separate companies and by rushing their products on the market at an alarming rate. Maywell had never fired anyone in its existence. Employees retired wealthy and few walked away. Maywell was a paranoia type company, no employee at the company was supposed to talk about company business outside of work. As far as Mr. Dannerman's case, board members did not want to deal with a disgruntled employee; especially someone like Mr. Dannerman who had access to some of Maywell's highly classified computer information. Board members along with company shareholders and investors appeased him by reassigning him to the board this would also to avoid public scrutiny.

When Mr. Dannerman reluctantly resigned under pressure he was so embarrassed he wanted to walk away, but he couldn't. Mr. Dannerman was a high roller, a risk taker, and a gambler. Mr. Dannerman obtained much of his wealth by trading stocks online.

In three years Mr. Dannerman invested millions of his Maywell stocks into a portfolio of more than forty million. He wined and dined at the world's finest attractions and casino's and won big. Hotel employees wouldn't dare tell anyone he dined, or had many of his trysts there because they wanted his business. But what goes up must come down and Mr. Dannerman's greed was eventually his downfall. The stock market crashed, he lost millions. He owed the IRS millions in unpaid taxes stemming from his enormous gains and winnings, which was the main reason he could not walk away.

Mr. Dannerman's mistakes were many, not to mention obvious. He showered his late mistress, Carol Flight with lavish gifts, cars, houses, furs, and jewelry. By showering Ms. Flight with all these lavish gifts, he waited too long to pay capital gains taxes on his earlier profits thinking Ms. Flight would pay for her fruits of labor or labor of love whatever you want to call it. Mr. Dannerman's biggest problem was his trading savvy, thinking he could outsmart investors. With the ego of the size of Texas, he thought he knew the stock market and traded stocks very aggressively. Instead of buying stock for future considerations, like retirement purposes, he bought it to support his lavish lifestyle.

At the time of Ms. Flight untimely death, stock trading became an obsession for Mr. Dannerman. There were rumors he showered Ms. Flight with lavish gifts to keep her quiet, hush money. Ms. Flight's partially nude body was found in a body bag by some fishermen on a small scale right outside Hilton Head, South Carolina. The autopsy report confirmed Ms. Flight was five months pregnant. Local authorities were investigating her execution style murder as mob related. Before her death, federal authorities were investigating Ms. Flight's wheeling and dealings because she was linked to some powerful people. Authorities combed through her office and home with a fine toothcomb looking for clues surrounding her death.

Ms. Flight was a beautiful seductive young woman who loved the finer things in life. She was caught in a web of deceit. She graduated with an MBA in finance from Rob Waller University with honors. Soon after, she started to work for a top investment firm on Wall Street and soon became one of its principals where she met Mr. Dannerman. Word had it she moved up the corporate latter by spending most of her time on her back. Mr. Dannerman was at the apex of his success, making an increasing number of trades on margin, money borrowed from a broker. This type of trading is considered by most financial analyst to be risky to say the least, but he didn't give a damn. It was all or nothing as far as he was concern. Ms. Flight loved risk takers, fell in love with Mr. Dannerman's stock trading prowess and he was infatuated and captured by her beauty. Instead of betting on mutual funds and bonds, their feelings were mutual which formed a dangerous and deadly bond.

·········

It was getting late and Nicole had finished her paperwork and checking her e-mail messages. She still had a lot of energy so she decided to read. She decided to finish reading Lawrence Sander's novel, *The Tenth Commandment,* she just finished reading John Grisham's book, *A Time to Kill.* Nicole loved reading, she was a lover of many books every since she was a little child. At the tender age of four, she was reading articles out of her mother's magazines lying around the house while her mother was cleaning up. Even before that, her mother would read to her when she was pregnant with Nicole. She had an assortment of books in her library from many different authors, ranging from Stephen King to the bible. Fact or fiction, it didn't matter, you name it she read it. She liked Terry McMillan books, *Mama and Disappearing Acts.* Especially *Disappearing Acts* because she could identify herself with Zora because they both had ambitions making it to the top in a male dominated world. She knew Terry wasn't a male basher as some give her credit for, but she thought it was interesting how big of a fool Franklin was in letting a good woman like Zora get away. Nicole was a firm believer that all is fair in love and war and to love someone, sometimes you have to actually let them go.

Robert would not have dared treated her, the way Franklin treated Zora in *Disappearing Acts.* Even though it was fiction, some women actually live the life that Zora lived. Nicole felt that people talk a lot, about things they do not know, especially when it comes to relationships. She also felt that men and women should have mutual respect for one another.

The stereo was playing Bony James song, *It's all Good.* Nicole was an average jazz and blues fan. She loved all types of music. In her mind, there are only two types of music, either its good or its bad. America categorizes music whereas Europe puts their music on one chart and goes strictly on record sales, which Nicole felt is the best way to dissect music. The phone ranged and it was Felicia and William Sharp, her old friends from college. They knew Nicole was at Martha's Vineyard because Nicole's mother told them Nicole would be there to take some time off before she started her duties at Maywell. They called Nicole's mother to get Nicole's number to congratulate her on becoming the new CEO at Maywell because they read about in *The Wall Street Journal.* Nicole's face was basically plastered on the front cover of all business magazines. This was history in the making.

"Hi Nicole, how are you doing?" they asked.

"Fine," said Nicole.

"We are calling to congratulate you. Your mother told us that you were on the island taking some time off and we will be on the island in a few days. It's been a long year and William and I decided to take a little time off ourselves for some much needed R&R."

Felicia was a top executive with Plasma Health Insurance in New York while William was owner and founder of his own mortgage firm. They all were good friends in college and all competed against one another for the highest grade point average. Call it vanity, but it created ambition.

"Oh Nicole by the way, we would like to invite you to a party some friends are having for Senator Al Gatewood of Massachusetts."

"Don't you mean fund-raiser." said Nicole.

They all had a big laugh.

"Actually you are right Nicole; it's for his re-election campaign."

"I will be more than happy to go to the party. Call me with the particulars when you arrive on the island said Nicole."

The party was at the country club. Nicole met and greeted everyone. Most of the people she was familiar with except senator Gatewood. Felicia introduced her to the senator. Senator Gatewood immediately recognized Nicole by her striking beauty. Senator Gatewood served in the Vietnam War and during that time he and Robert became close friends. Robert always talked about her from sun up to sundown because Nicole was the apple of his eye. Robert could not help himself as he constantly showed off Nicole's picture to everyone he met. The senator and the comrades were sick to their stomachs of hearing Robert talk about Nicole. But after finally meeting her he understood why

Robert went on and on pining over Nicole. The senator and Robert were close as nineteen is to twenty and shared many secrets just in case one of them did not make it back home. The senator always reiterated to Robert that he wanted to get involved in politics and wanted to serve his home state of Massachusetts. He and Robert both served time in the Air Force. The two were the most patriotic men you ever wanted to meet.

"Senator Gatewood, this is Nicole," said Felicia.

"Hi Nicole, nice to meet you, I heard so many good things about you, said the Senator."

"The pleasure is all mine", said Nicole.

"Nicole, pardon me for staring. I don't want to make you feel uncomfortable or anything of that nature."

"No not at all," said Nicole.

Even though she caught the senator staring at her, he did not startle her because she was use to men staring at her, not vanity, just fact.

"Nicole the reason I was staring at you is because I feel I already know you, literally speaking."

"But senator, we've just actually met."

"I know." said the senator.

Nicole's antenna really went up. Is this man some sort of freak of nature? She thought to herself, but gave him the benefit of the doubt. She was interested in what the senator had to say, so were Felicia and William.

"You see Nicole, I'm a Vietnam Veteran, and during that time your husband, Robert and I became close friends. I was the last person to see him alive."

Nicole's heart was in her mouth and she almost actually fainted, she almost dropped her drink, but kept her composure. She was very interested in what the senator had to say.

"Nicole, Robert truly loved you. He used to write love letters to you everyday, even though he could not mail them. He slept with your picture by his side every night and longed for his return to the States just to be with you."

Nicole looked in amazement; she knew Robert loved her without a doubt, but wanted the senator to continue.

"Nicole, that's why I was staring at you so, Robert used to show pictures of you to me and the rest of the crew everyday. Those pictures do not do you justice because you are more beautiful in person than any picture Robert ever showed us. Robert was never the one to lie, but you are more beautiful than he said you were. Nicole, Robert and I went through some tough times together and we confided in one another for moral support. We were like family, fraternal brothers in the heat of the battle. It was a jungle over there in Nam."

"I can image," said Nicole.

"But Robert was never the one to back down or shy away from a challenge. Robert accepted his responsibilities as a man and faced it head on. He wanted the war to end so he could return home and start a family. I wanted to meet with you after I returned from Nam, but I just could not face you. Plus, my head was all messed up. When I returned home I didn't know if I was coming or going. I had many issues to deal with. Its difficult to face anyone who just lost someone they truly loved."

"That was Robert alright," said Nicole.

"That's one of the main reason I wanted to get involved in politics so I could help change the laws concerning how Vietnam Veterans were unfairly treated once that came back home." the senator said.

"Senator Gatewood, what actually happened to Robert, the circumstances surrounding his death were unclear? What were his last days like?" said Nicole.

"Nicole are you sure you want to drag up old wounds, I know you want to know, but I think its time to put some kind of closure concerning Robert's death." said Felicia.

"Felicia I'm strong enough to handle it after all these years, but I couldn't get hardly any information concerning Robert death. The little information I did received I had to go through a bunch of red tape, the everlasting chain of bureaucracy and I still don't anymore now than I knew back then when this whole investigation started," said Nicole.

"Yes I know you are strong Nicole, but the only thing you really need to know is that Robert loved you."

"I know that Felicia, I just want to get the facts straight from a credible source without going through top bureaucrats on Capitol Hill."

"Well Nicole these are the facts as I actually know them. Robert lived every day to the fullest. We ran an air raid at night to attack and destroy a Vietnamese weapon facility where we were informed they were making nuclear weapons and biochemicals for future terrorist attacks and Robert's fighter plane was shot down. Robert plane was found, but his body was not. Reports insinuated that the Vietnamese refugees found and tortured Robert to death. We do not officially know if Robert ejected from the plane before the plane actually went down. All we know is he was missing and there was no sign of his body."

Nicole cringed at the thought of Robert's body being tortured, how brutal. It made her sick in the stomach. Robert treated his body like a temple. He had the six- pack abs, the whole nine yards. All she could think about when it came to Robert's body was how his body gently caressed her body. His simple touch made her fingers and toes curl up. It was as though she had an outer body experience when he touched her. Robert didn't need any instructions he knew how to turn her on. Robert knew her worth.

"Do you think there is a strong possibility that he may have survived this brutal attack?" asked Nicole.

"Anything is a possibility, because Robert had a strong will. Robert was willing to die for his country. Even though the Vietnamese were fearless and did not have a conscience whatsoever, no regard for human life. They sacrificed and were offering up kids. The Vietnamese kids were strapped with bombs on their persons and walked directly into enemy territory. Many people lost their lives when those bombs exploded. It was a sad case to see. Worst than anything you will ever read in a Stephen King's novel. Death did not discriminate in Nam. We were prepared and literally programmed to die and didn't even think about ever setting foot on U.S. soil again." said senator Gatewood.

"Senator, I have read many reports and have seen many TV specials about POW's and MIA's who were presumed dead, but have taken on new identities in Southeast Asia in these so-called concentration camps. Do you think this could have been a possibility with the circumstances surrounding Robert's death." said Felicia?

"Felicia you're grasping at straws, said Nicole. If Robert were alive I'm sure the United States government would have record, dog tags or something concerning POW's and MIA's wouldn't they senator?" said Nicole.

"Well Nicole there is always a marginal room for error, but the United States government has done everything possible in keeping record of POW's and MIA's." said the senator.

"I know the government hasn't exhausted all their resources and efforts concerning POW's and MIA's. To me it seems like more could be done because their love ones are still in limbo," said William.

"You got that right," said Felicia.

"As far as I'm concerned, they haven't scratched the surface," said William.

The senator knew that wasn't true. The government had made significant strides surrounding POW's and MIA's cases even though a lot more could be done, but people are entitled to their own opinions. The senator also knew people like to vent their frustrations outwardly.

"Nicole I always wanted to get in touch with you and tell you about the circumstances concerning Robert's death and that you were constantly on his mind. In fact, he wanted me to ensure you that he loved you more today than he did yesterday. As each day passed, he just fell in love with you over and over again. The love he had for you motivated him to make it through the war. The memories I have are painful to this day. I could not face you."

The senator reached under his French cuff shirt and gave Nicole a bracelet that belonged to Robert. He did not want to part with it because Robert gave it to him as a token of their fraternal brotherhood during the war. Under normal circumstances, he would not dare part with it, but felt compelled that Nicole should have it.

"Nicole, Robert gave this bracelet to me in case he didn't make it back from the war. I am now giving it to you. It shows you how close of a bond we formed in Nam. You will find more use for it than I will. The memories that we shared in Nam still rings fresh in my mind. I know Robert's spirit is alive inside you, but now you have something physical, something to touch as well. Something to explain the spirit a person has in their heart, a sacred love two people share."

The senator gave Nicole the bracelet along with a picture of the both of them took in Nam. It was as though Robert had not aged, maybe a few gray hairs here and there. Nicole was about to burst into tears, but managed to maintain her composure. She hugged and thanked the senator. It was as though Robert was staring her directly in the face. The love they shared, went far beyond the physical, it was a spiritual thing.

The party was almost over and the drive back to the house was a somber one, but at the same time fulfilling. Nicole held and squeezed the bracelet ever so tight as though the bracelet had life.

"Nicole, say something", said Felicia.

"I'm okay, really, I just have a lost for words." said Nicole.

"Honey leave her alone, give her some time and space, said William.

"That's just like Robert, always stealing the show," Nicole said with a laugh.

"You most admit it was some party." said Felicia.

"You got that right, I am glad you guys invited me because I really did not feel like socializing tonight." said Nicole.

The car drove up in front of the beach house and Nicole got out of the car dropped her purse. She was so jittery; she was shaking like a leaf on a tree as she was searching for her keys in the dark.

"Nicole, are you sure you are alright? You know you are welcome to stay with us tonight. Come over at least for a night cap." said Felicia.

"Thanks guys, as I said earlier I'm alright. Plus, I've got an early morning flight." said Nicole.

They exchanged pleasantries along with their telephone numbers and addresses. They vowed to keep in touch with one another. They all agreed that they would be there for one another and promised to get together more often.

It was morning and Nicole made it through the night and what a rough night to say the least. She had butterflies in her stomach all night. Thoughts about Robert kept dancing in her head, hoping he might still be alive. Could there be any shred of evidence that Robert may be alive? "No, it's been too long a voice said." You would have heard something by now wouldn't you think." She was always taught at a tender young age to go to school, get a good education, get a good job, get married, have kids, and live happily ever after. Hell three out of five isn't bad. Anyone would be happy to accomplish that kind of feat, not Nicole, a perfectionist who thrived on the great American dream. Damn how could something so right go so wrong? She was angry not to mention bitter. She had questions, but no answers. Then all these scenarios started playing out in her mind. "Who is responsible for this? Is it God?" How could God let something so great turn so tragic? She felt in her heart and mind that God is love, but the only love she ever knew was gone. It doesn't make sense; it just doesn't add up. She didn't want to question God because that wouldn't be too wise. Her parents told her as a child, God is not going to put more on you than you can handle even though she never understood this religion thing, which she considers to be a great mystery. For the many times she read the bible she was confused. It seemed to her at some point her intelligence should have intervened and figure out the bible "Should she throw rocks at the sky?" a voice said. This kind of thing has been going on a lot lately, questioning her self, over and over again. Something inside her told her to stop it, just stop it Nicole before you have a nervous breakdown. My mind is not playing tricks on me. She could not come to grips with Robert's death so it seemed. Robert's death was a constant reminder. It was like a burning sensation that burns deep in the guts that would not go away. She knew she would never get over Robert, but thoughts of Robert being alive after all these years were ridiculous.

Her flight back to Orangeburg was a long flight, mixed emotions everywhere. She felt she better get it together fast because she had a major company to run. She felt Robert would want it this way, telling her to get on with her life. But wait no one has ever spoken with a dead man. This job is to be the cure all of all cure alls, right. "I don't think so," said a voice that came from within.

CHAPTER 3

The executive wing on the third floor was professionally plush, office space that only a true professional could appreciate. It was pure royalty. There was a conference room filled with expensive mahogany and glass furniture. On the north end, there was a glamorous restaurant called the Executive Club overlooking a lake and botanic gardens. Now, the Executive Club is where Maywell's executives took their guests to conduct business, the club was a networking mecca.

Ty Dannerman still occupied the second largest office space in the complex while Nicole had the largest; his office was complemented by awards Maywell had accomplished during his reign as CEO. He was slim built with a tall frame. He dressed for success. He kept a band-aid in his pocket because he was so sharp he was afraid he might cut himself. The suits he wore; a person could not find in the store. The material his suits were made of a person found hard to pronounce.

At Nicole's presentation to the board, he almost stole the show because board members were teasing him that he missed his calling, becoming a model. He thought this was great that he found favor with the board. His attire was extravagant. They went as far to say that he was a walking billboard for a top designer. After the meeting the left the office in a hurry, this was nothing new to the board members even though Nicole thought it was strange. He would leave early on some days to have a tryst with

Ms. Flight. He left in such a hurry one would have thought that someone was after him. When he was CEO he was always so evasive, a dictator, which rubbed some board members the wrong way. He informed his secretary he was gone for the day and rushed off in his new white pearl Lexus. He picked up his cellular phone and informed the person on the other end that he would be there shortly. His destination, Elloree, South Carolina on Lake Marion is where he was to meet his confidant or concubine.

At Lake Marion he went to a secluded area of the park where someone directly approached him. That someone was none other than Arthur McRand, the CEO of Conquest Computers, Maywell's biggest competitor. They didn't want to take the risk of being seen in public. Art had flown up from Conquest corporate headquarters in Atlanta.

"Ty, I see you finally came to your senses," said Art.

"Art you are a smart man you know these kind of things take time," said Ty.

"Hell I thought you had forgotten about me Ty. That you weren't serious about your plan".

"Art you know me by now. When it comes to money, I'm always serious. If it doesn't make dollars it doesn't make sense."

Ty and Art had been acquaintances for a while since they ran in the same circles, networking with the same clients, going after the same market. One could hardly call them friends because they were rivals trying to destroy one another because the bottom line is the almighty dollar. Ty contacted Art about a deadly game of espionage, a game that could destroy Maywell Electronics after he was ousted as CEO. It was payback time for Ty. His heart was literally filled with bitterness after being forced to resign as Maywell's CEO.

Mr. McRand is a religious fanatic. He always preached of having a vision for Conquest Computers. That Conquest would become the number one computer company in the next millennium and that he would do what ever it takes even if it kills him to keep the legacy of his grandfather alive. He told the employers at Conquest that a corporation today cannot thrive without having a vision of its long-term goals. He went to church services all the time with his family. Mr. McRand didn't dare impart his religious beliefs on his employees because religion and politics just don't mix. He didn't want to come off as a hypocrite, but for the most part he kept his religious belief to himself at the workplace. But if a person walked into his office they could tell he was a religious fanatic with bibles and pictures of the bible and its verses imprinted everywhere you turned in his office. He had a plaque on his desk that read, "God I know you will take care of my problems today so I will just sit back and smile and let you take care of them". He was a devout family man, a hell of a provider whose family wanted for nothing. His kids went to the best school's money could provide. Hell, they could have bought the school if they wanted. His wife didn't work. She provided money to local charities and played bridge with her friends. They had the best of everything. Mr. McRand was at the stage of his life now that everything he accumulated was just gravy. He was listed in the top fifty in Forbes magazine as one of the wealthiest people in the world.

"Art, I'm so pissed off at them bastards at Maywell, I could murder them all."

"Yeah I know you could, but that would be letting them SOB's off easy, make their ass suffer," said Art.

"I would like to wipe that smug look off their face permanently", said Ty.

"What better way to accomplish that, you hit them where it hurts, their pockets, by making a damn fool out of them," said Art.

"I feel you as they say in the hip hop world," said Ty.

"Ty don't be speaking that damn jargon to me."

"Art, I'm so damn mad at those spineless bastards, they didn't even have the guts to tell me to my face they wanted me to step down. They kept pressuring me and pressuring me to resign. Those bastards had the audacity to send me an e-mail message, a damn e-mail message. Can you believe that shit, a damn e-mail message after all the effort I put into that damn company, to make it the number one computer company in the world. That's the fucking thanks I get. Art, can you imagine how humiliated I felt, replacing me with a woman. That was John Aslong's doing. That bastard hates my guts. I bet that SOB slept with Nicole. What has this damn world come too? Society has taking this equal rights shit too damn far. There was a time a woman's place was defined to the kitchen and the bedroom, laying flat on their backs. Now they lay on their backs to move up the corporate latter. Some how they got in their heads they can do just as good of a job as a man. I use to pay all the bills and I came home one day and my wife said she wanted to pay them and that I would have to start giving her my money, not just an allowance, isn't that some shit. When all she would do is sit at home and watch those damn fucking soap operas. It's those damn women activist groups that what's messing up every damn thing. The man was responsible for bringing home the bacon and giving them spending money. Now they think they can take on the world. What's next, the White House? That will be the day. This is straight up bullshit. Maywell will pay. They pacified my ass by reassigning me to the board. I was caught behind the eight ball, in a difficult situation because I just can't walk away. Not now anyway until I get my house in order."

"Ty, Maywell don't want you to walk away, not right now anyway. You somewhat remain a valuable asset to them. They want to continue to use your expertise so you won't due them any harm, by taking them to court, all the more reason to screw there assess. They want the dust to settle and when it does believe me, they will let your ass ride quietly into the sunset. They will have no more use for your ass. Do until them what others have done unto you, literally. Fight fire with fire. There is a silver lining to all this, you get to rebuild your portfolio and if you play this right you can make a killing. You can make enough money so that your grandchildren's future generation would be set for life and at the same time destroy those pompous bastards at Maywell. What better way to get revenge, two-fold, you humiliate their ass and destroy them at the same time. Look at the overall picture. You said Ms. Gershom came in with a very astute business plan. Keep your cool and use it to your advantage. Hell we all can profit from this if we play our cards right," said Art.

"Replacing me with a woman, I would just like to wipe that smug look off her damn face. I would just like to; you know put her in her proper place." said Ty.

"Wait a minute Ty, wait one damn minute. I know Nicole is beautiful and all, but you have to think with your top head, not the bottom one if you know what I mean, if we want to pull this off. We got too much riding on this. Don't go messing everything up because you have some over active hormones. You got plenty of time for that shit. That's what got you in the shape you're in now, where you cannot just walk away. You're not the first man this has happened to and you certainly won't be the last. This sort of thing has been going on since the beginning of time. Women can be so seductive and enticing that it makes us lose our focus and go completely out of our damn minds. Hell why do you think they are shaped the way they are?

The playing field had to be equaled somehow because if it wasn't we men would just bulldoze right over them with our caveman mentality," said Art.

There was a moment of silence as the sun was going down in the cool of the day. Both men had an agenda to destroy Maywell. Especially for Art, the pain goes much deeper. It wasn't about the money. It was personal. Sure he wanted Conquest to become the number one computer company in the world, it was his family dream. Art had a more personal agenda to destroy Maywell. Art blamed old man Maywell for the death of his grandfather, Jim McRand, whom he loved dearly. His grandfather and old man Maywell's had a running feud worst than the Hatfield's and the McCoy's. Old man Maywell and McRand went into business together making electronic devices. They were best of friends growing up and vowed to make a better life for themselves unlike their forefathers. Old man Maywell considered himself to be the smarter of the two was the front man while McRand was more like the silent partner running the day-to-day operations. He was the one that kept the business afloat. He was not a people person. People in the industry thought that old man Maywell was the sole proprietor because he was the one always out in front, marketing the business. He was good, very good. So good that he could sell you your own shirt, off your back. The difference between the two men was like night and day. Old man Maywell wanted the finer things in life while McRand was satisfied in just being comfortable with what life dealt him. He was a hell of a provider; his family depended on him dearly.

Old man Maywell wanted to expand the business and saw a bigger picture and wanted more than a mom and pop operation. McRand was content in running a small-scale operation, old man Maywell knew he couldn't expand unless McRand actually agreed to it because the partnership was split fifty, fifty. He got McRand to sign a bogus contract that made him the sole proprietor. This was the straw that broke McRand's back when he eventually found out what old man Maywell had done. He trusted him totally. He couldn't understand how a man considered to be a friend could be so treacherous, a man he had known his entire life. McRand never recovered, he was financially ruined which eventually lead to his death and started a forever long lasting feud between the two families.

It was Art who dreamed of following in his grandfather's footsteps. He saw through the years of the bad blood between the families and vowed to take vengeance one day. Now the day of retribution has finally arrived and he planned to get back what was rightfully his. He wanted to make his grandfather proud and make old man Maywell turn over in his grave.

The plan was put in motion where it was carefully thought out. The first step was to use Mr. Dannerman's expertise to tap into Maywell's computer banks where the company's top secret and confidential files are kept. Carefully bugging Maywell's system whether it was voice activated or e-mail systems, a stone wouldn't be left unturned. Conquest would have access to some of Maywell's secret files. They would be able to retrieve and monitor every conversation and message. Knowing when deals are made. Conquest would be able to undermine Maywell. Ty would have to keep his wits about him and treat Nicole with respect. He knew the lady was astute and knowledgeable if he could just play into her hands. Nicole had entered into a league with the big boys. It's no longer fun and games, its crunch time and Maywell will forever suffer the consequences. He would have to give up his own ambitions in order to gain power.

CHAPTER 4

Nicole picked her mother's up from the airport around two o'clock p.m. eastern standard time. Her mother had promised Nicole she would pay her a visit once Nicole had settled and moved in her new house. They were happy to see one another as they hugged and embraced each other endlessly at the airport. It had only been six months since they had seen one another, but it seemed like a lifetime.

Nicole grabbed her mother luggage, as her mother looked at Nicole with pride and admiration. She could not help but to stare, checking Nicole out from head to toe. It's a mother's intuition to make sure their child is okay. She was so proud of Nicole and wished that her late husband was there to see his lovely daughter. It brought tears to her eyes, but she would not dare let Nicole see her cry. She knew Nicole's father always knew this day would come. He taught Nicole not to let her gender be a liability in life, but an asset. Her father drove Nicole and he often stated that a person could pull themselves up by their own bootstraps if they are determined. He told Nicole, "the word can't, shouldn't be in her vocabulary."

They arrived at Nicole's house and while they were pulling up in the driveway, Nicole's mother was astonished. She could not believe how beautiful Nicole's house was. The lawn was like a golf course, manicured to perfection. The beautiful trees and garden looked like the Garden of Eden. All and all, the property was a ponderosa with flowers blooming everywhere sitting on thirteen acres.

Nicole's mother had not seen anything this beautiful in her life. Sure, she had read about places like this, but could not image anything like this in her wildest dreams. To be close with Mother Nature was the main reason she felt people in the north was returning to the south. She had some fond memories of the south as a child, but felt she needed a change of scenery as a teenager and moved up north.

She admired Nicole's furniture. The tables and floors had a high gloss along with the chairs, chests, cupboards, and beds. This was the work of a craftsman, not an interior decorator, she thought. She opened the widow and smelled the sweet aroma of azaleas, camellias, roses, and the Carolina jasmines, the state flower, in full bloom. She saw some Carolina wrens in the trees chirping.

She hurried to unpack because Nicole had made dinner reservations at the country club. She was famished and was anxious to get to the country club. Nicole had told her how beautiful the establishment was. This would truly be a mother and daughter night out. They both felt this is what life is all about, being together with your family. Especially, since family values have all but eroded. Kids taking firearms to school and killing one another, these types of incidents use to be unheard of. The drugs, the violence, that are terrorizing our community. You hear all about these horror stories on the evening news. Crack use to be something a person stepped over walking on the sidewalk or street, now it is an epidemic in our society. When will the madness stop?

Nicole's mother was very fortunate that Nicole did not have to experience these issues that are plaguing our society today. Charity begins at home, Nicole was a goodly child growing up, did not give her parents any problems whatsoever. They sat her down at an early age and told her about the birds and the bees, no holds barred. Nicole was special, but all kids should be special to their parents. Nicole's parents did their best in rearing her and preparing her for life. Nothing in this lifetime could have prepared Nicole for what she has been through since Robert's death. No preparation in the world could ever have done that. Nicole's parents told her that things that do not kill you will make you stronger.

At the country club, Nicole introduced her mother to some of her co-workers along with staff members at the club. They could all see where Nicole inherited her beauty. Her mother was also a looker in her day. Hell, even until this day she is fair to look at. She looked young for her age. Nicole's father use to tell her stories on how her mother's striking beauty mesmerized him when they first met and how he literally wooed her into marrying him.

Over dinner, they engaged in some small talk. Nicole's mother informed her that Andrea, Nicole's childhood friend had called to inform her that she was five months pregnant. Nicole just stared into space as though she was in a trance. Her mother figured Nicole must to have been thinking about the family she never had with Robert. Nicole's mother could identify what Nicole was feeling because her second, a daughter, was still born at birth. Nicole would have a little sister if the baby had lived. At that point she and Nicole's father had given up on having any more kids. They didn't want to deal with the emotional trauma. Nicole's mothers knew how Nicole and Andrea carried on as kids and still do until this day. Nicole finally answered and said that it was great that Andrea was pregnant for the umpteenth time. Nicole felt Andrea was the most fertile woman she ever knew. It seemed as though Andrea's husband could just look at her and Andrea would become pregnant. Andrea reminded her of the life she never had with Robert.

On the way home there wasn't two words said. Moreover, when they arrived at Nicole's house to retire for the night, her mother could not take it anymore.

"Nicole honey, what's wrong"? said her mother.

"Oh nothing mother, I'm just a little tired that's all", said Nicole.

"Nicole, come on, you have to get up very early in the morning to fool me, and a mother knows these things. So come on, what is it? You have been preoccupied ever since you picked me up from the airport. You were quiet over dinner and did not say two words on the way home. Is every thing okay with your job?"

"Really mother, its nothing, I'm just a little tired from the jet lag coming back from Martha's Vineyard."

"Don't give me that tired stuff, I know better. I know the difference from being tired and being preoccupied," her mother said.

Nicole eyes got watery.

"Mother I could never fool you could I."

"Nicole I knew you when you were forming in my womb. I use to talk and sing to you each day when I found out I was pregnant with you."

Nicole wanted to cry as she put her head in her mother's lap, but she did not want her mother to see her that way so she remained strong. She had cried herself to sleep many nights.

"So Nicole what's wrong? Will I have to drag it out of you? said her mother.

"No mother, you don't have to drag it out of me, but it would be nice if you sing to me like you use to do before bedtime," Nicole said with a laugh.

"You know I certainly enjoyed singing to you when you were a child," her mother said.

"Mother I didn't want to say anything to anyone because I didn't want anyone to think I was losing my mind."

There was a pause.

"No dear, anyone who knows you knows you aren't crazy by any stretch of the imagination."

Nicole took a deep breath and tried to fight back the tears. Her mother took her in her arms, and patted her on the back and squeezed her hand. This episode brought back memories when they use to have their little girlie talks when Nicole was a child. Nicole had her full attention.

"Mother I found out some conflicting information about the circumstances surrounding Robert's death when I was at Martha's Vineyard."

"Nicole".

"Wait a minute mother before you say anything. I not still pining over the circumstances concerning Robert's death, I'm just trying to understand the situation, that's all", said Nicole.

"That's a relief; I don't wont you to get depressed all over again about this. I know it's hard but at some point and time you have to let go." said her mother.

"Senator Gatewood of Massachusetts who I had the opportunity to meet while I was at Martha's Vineyard was a close friend of Robert's during the Vietnam War; he was the last person who saw Robert alive."

Her mother had a pale look on her face but remained calm as though she had seen a ghost.

"Senator Gatewood informed me that Robert's body was never found when his plane was shot down during the night raid, but the debris from Robert's plane was found. The worst case scenario is that Robert's body was brutally tortured by scavenges."

"Nicole what are you trying to say. That it is a strong possibility that Robert may be alive. Honey, do not put yourself through that again. You have fought that battle already."

"Mother all I'm saying is what the senator told me. Do not read too much into it. There will always be uncertainty concerning those who fought in the war. All I am saying is what the senator told me. That's Robert's remains were not found. I have more information now than I did before concerning Robert's death. Look mother, the senator gave me this beautiful bracelet that Robert gave him during the war."

Her mother was at a lost for words. She had that concern look of a mother looking out for their child. She knew the pain and suffering Nicole had been through which almost landed her daughter in a mental institution. She had hoped that these wounds were healed, but now it seemed as though salt had been poured into them. She knew the families of those soldiers who fought in the war had a rough time since the war and will forever endure the pain and heartache.

"Mother say something", said Nicole.

"Sweetie I'm at a lost for words. I know how important this is to you. It's always tough on a person who has lost a love one. So, what's the story? What are you going to do"?

"Mother it more than a story. It goes much deeper than that. I want to bring closure to this situation and every time I come close, I get hit with a bombshell. Robert was the love of my life and not a single day goes by that I do not think about or dream about the family we could have had. I have tried everything in my power to move on. I indulged myself in my career trying to move on, but nothing has worked. At this stage of my life I definitely don't need any distractions."

"Nicole if you want to stand up and continue to fight for the love of your life that's fine, if you feel that strongly about it. But if you can't be chastised by the challenges of love in some cases which means losing a love one you don't have anything to be proud of, because if you can't stand up for the equality of love you're not in love anyway."

"Mother, you knew how much I loved Robert; we were soul mates just like you and daddy. I look at you and try to draw strength from you because you are a strong woman. I was there and know what you went through when daddy died. You were strong. I just wish I could be as strong as you are because I know how much daddy meant to you and how well you handled his death."

"We are talking about different manifestation, but the same principle. Your father was ill, and had lived to a ripe old age. He had weathered the storm and was ready to die plus we had you. Robert was at the prime of his life even though he wasn't afraid to die and you had no kids. I know you must feel cheated in some respect, but that's the way life is, we cannot always write a perfect script. I am behind you one hundred percent. If you need me I'm here for you."

"Am I fighting a lost cause mother," said Nicole.

"Not at all honey, if its ninety-nine point nine percent then there is a window of opportunity of point one percent then you have to go after that one percent. To fight for love or to be loved is never a lost cause my dear. Moreover, a person never dies if you cherish the memories of that person in your heart and in your mind. Love is spirit and spirit never dies, you preserve it."

"Mother, its not like I don't want to preserve the love I had for Robert it's the circumstances surrounding his death that's so challenging. I have opened a new chapter in my life. I'm dedicated to my career as being CEO of Maywell Electronics and I can't lose my focus. I have too much riding on this and a lot of people counting on me. It's just bad timing right now."

"Then make time, Nicole honey, its time for you to set your priorities straight. With your credentials, you can always find another job, but you have had only one true love in your life and that was Robert. I know you have finally accomplished your dream in becoming CEO of a major corporation, but what is more important to you? Knowing you like I do you will not be satisfied until you know for sure the circumstances concerning Robert's death. You will always be wondering what if. And that's no way to live your life wondering what if."

"You are right mother. There is no way I can be at peace with myself until I am one hundred percent certain. I am hesitant because the situation would be very cumbersome to me and would eventually affect my work not to mention my sanity."

"Nicole, honey you can do both. I have all the confidence in the world in you. You can work and still pursue information surrounding Robert's death. What did the senator and your friend suggest you do?"

"They thought I should look into it and research it further. Felicia was very adamant about it and the senator said he would help me in anyway he could."

"Well at least he can help you cut through all the red tape on Capitol Hill."

"Working with the senator should save me some time that's for sure so that I won't have to concentrate all of my time and efforts on this matter. Looking at this bracelet fuels my desire to pursue this mother."

"I know that you mention earlier that Robert gave it to him during the war."

"Robert and the senator made some sort of pact out of brotherly love in case one of them didn't make back home that they will each have something to remember one another."

"That's interesting."

"Senator Gatewood was one of Robert's closest friends. He's from Boston. He joined the Air Force a few yeas before Robert was named lieutenant. He was a great leader, a person who was admired among his peers. Probably the nicest man I know besides Robert. He is a very interesting individual. He told me how much Robert talked about me and couldn't wait to get back home."

"That's great, now call him," said her mother.

"I will, but first I will take a few days off while the board implements my plans and show you some of the state's historical sites. Mother Nature has been very kind to South Carolina," said Nicole.

"You don't have to do that Nicole. I know you have a lot of irons in the fire. I'm just glad we can finally spend some time together, I miss you dearly," said her mother.

"Mother, please do not even try it. It's the least I can do especially since you came so far to be with me."

"Well it would be nice just to get out, said her mother.

The next morning, they packed a lunch heading south towards Charleston, South Carolina. South Carolina is so beautiful this time of the year. Nicole took the scenic route as they stopped and ate lunch at one to the state's beautiful botanic gardens. The scenery made the state's flag issues seemed minimal even though it is a hot topic. They passed by beautiful neighborhoods where upper class America dwelled. They took pictures of beautiful homes, landscapes, and historic sites. The sunlight beamed through the sunroof as the sky was clear on this sunny spring-like day. The birds were singing, but they could not hear them because Nicole had her stereo tuned up louder than usual. The flowers and trees were in full ascension. Cattle grazed the fields as they drove past tobacco row.

Nicole's mother was taken away by some of the state's natural resources, like the large forests and the abundance of wildlife, not to mention the farmland that occupies half of the state. She had forgotten how beautiful life could actually be. She had grown accustomed to the rat race of the city. She felt a sense of freedom, for an instance she thought about moving to South Carolina to be near Nicole. She realized this part of the country provided a good wholesome living, a place to raise kids, an environment to protect them from the dangers of urban violence like gangs and drugs that has robbed so many young lives.

There was not a doubt in her mind why Nicole had made the choice in relocating to this part of the country and it was not just for the money. "Thank you God", her mother said to herself as she gazed through the sunroof. She was not a religious fanatic by any stretch of the imagination, but she knew the powers to be was looking out for her daughter. It had to be because how else could you explain it, especially if you've been through the things Nicole had been through and still live to tell about it.

As they were getting gas, Nicole thought about Robert and how Robert used to take good care of his car. He always stated, "If you take care of your car it will take care of you." Nicole really did not grasp what Robert was talking about at the time, but he was simply stating to her to use one type of gas and oil in your car. Robert took care of everything he owned; he was just that type of a guy. Nicole filled up the gas tank and got some bottled water as her mother bought a pack of gum.

"Mother we should arrive in Charleston shortly."

"Believe me I am in no hurry. I am just amazed that Mother Nature can be so beautiful. I wish your father and I could have lived in a place like this when you were growing up."

"But mother I'm here now, better late than never right. Plus, I thought you said daddy didn't like this part of the country especially since it was the south."

"It wasn't the south your father didn't like. It was just what the south or this part of the country represented the mentality of the people. Case in point the flag issue here."

"Mother when you say mentality, are you talking about prejudice?"

"Somewhat, you know the people in the south moved north for a better way of life. The opportunities were a lot better in the north than the south. People wanted to work in factories not the fields. Many people had to quit school in order to support their families. After the civil war and the civil rights movement, the south was not the same. At the time the south seemed so chaotic."

"Mother I especially know now that all people are created equal. Look at me now, a women being CEO of a major corporation. Years ago it would have been unheard of, a woman in a male dominate field. A person's color or gender should not be a handicap because none of us are responsible for being here. I know there is always room for improvement, but mother haven't we have made tremendous strides in race relations and gender equality laws?"

"Sure we have, but what I'm saying is that we shouldn't have to have laws in the first place to make people do the right thing. It should come from the heart."

"You think daddy would have changed his mind if times were like they are now."

"No your father stuck by his beliefs and rightfully so".

So daddy was pretty adamant that he didn't want to have anything to do with the south because of certain prejudices and what it represented."

"That's putting it mildly because no one is born prejudice. Prejudice is taught and reared in a child." We raised you to see a person's character not their color. Prejudice comes in many different forms, not just the texture of a person's skin or male against female. Prejudice exists in a way we interact with one another, the way we look and the way we talk."

"We have to as individuals come to the realization that we can accomplish so much more if we all could just get pass this racial barrier."

"Never, not in this life time, it's a great concept, but people can only be who they are and that's comes from within. Simply put its just plain ignorance. We raised you to treat every individual like you would treat yourself. Moreover, if you truly cared for yourself then you would never have a problem in getting along with anyone. Nicole you are without color, neither white nor black without any particular origin. That's the way we raised you and if you see everyone else that way than you will see that all people are created equal. It may seem hard to believe. If one could hear our conversation now without actually seeing us they would automatically think we are of a particular race. All of our blood is red. There should be no such thing as race; just people and we all should respect that. Yeah, some things have gotten better since I was a child, but for the most part we still have a long way to go. I just feel that instead of waking up we just rolled over. Check on a job application that you are of no particular origin and see if you get the job. They will think you are some freak of nature. They also want you to fill out an affirmative action questionnaire by telling you its voluntary, why? I tell you why, just for statistical data? When the most experienced person should get the job, color shouldn't matter, but it does. Case in point if someone was listening to our conversation we are having right now without seeing us they would automatically think we were black," said her mother.

"Mother Robert and I shared the same beliefs as you and daddy when it comes to love and respect. A person should always respect his fellow man."

They arrived at the hotel in Charleston. The parking attendant took Nicole's keys. They unpacked and freshen up before Nicole ordered room service. They were road weary and neither felt like going out for dinner. They wanted to have a nice quiet evening and engaged in some small talk for tomorrow would be a day for sightseeing. Nicole wanted to catch up on her reading because all she had been reading lately were business reports and financial statements. Reading gave her serenity. She felt you do not have to actually visit a place, by reading it takes you there. The power of imagination can be a powerful force if you let it. Nicole's favorite subject was romance because she was a true romantic. When Robert and she first got married, Robert had an air about him that drove her crazy. Forty ways to be exact as she vividly remembers topped off with candy, flowers, and candlelit dinners.

Robert's whole intellect, the way he would caress her shoulders and gently stroke her down her back use to send chills down her spine. The way he uses to seduce her with his big brown eyes. His smile with dimples as deep as the Mississippi River was so alluring, all these things she could remember as they cuddled up near the fireplace.

The next morning Nicole rose up at six o'clock a.m. to go on her daily morning jog as her mother slept peacefully. On the way out the door Nicole kissed her mother on her cheek as she stared for a moment and realized how blessed she really is to have a mother like hers. Nicole felt Mother's Day was every day because mothers are truly special and should be treated with the up most respect, for she had lost the man in her life, which she truly adored and wanted to spend as much time as she could with her mother. Her mother was her source of strength since Robert's death and she depended heavily on her mother. She wanted her mother to move in with her but she knew her mother wasn't going to go for that because her mother felt Nicole had to spread her on wings, to be her own person.

When she returned from her jog her mother was watching The Today Show.

"I see some things never change," said Nicole as she was drinking some bottled water while wiping away the perspiration on her face.

"And what do you mean by that young lady."

"I see The Today Show is still one of your favorite television programs."

"And what's wrong with that. It's informative and plus I'm interested in world affairs."

"World affairs my foot, only affair you are interested in is having an affair with Mr. Smooth."

"Oh I see you still have your wits about you. Can I help it if he presents the news like no other anchor? Plus, I like his interviewing skills."

"Funny how you would use the word skills and Mr. Smooth in the same sentence mother."

"Don't get beside yourself young lady; I'm still your mother."

They had a big laugh because Nicole liked to tease her mother about Mr. Smooth. She knew her mother was a huge Mr. Smooth fan because he reminded her mother of her father. They had the same personality. Her mother didn't watch too much

TV unless it was The Ophrah Winstone Show or The Today Show. Her mother loved Ophrah, Mr. Smooth, and Dan Rathmore. Nicole's mother felt Mr. Smooth had been getting a bad rap as many considered him to be arrogant. She felt he was misunderstood, the man is confident in his abilities and she respected him for that, but realized some people considered the two words as having the same meaning.

"Mother are you ready to eat" because I am famished, said Nicole as she was getting out of the shower.

"Do you have any place special in mind", said her mother.

"Yeah, the desk clerk gave me this brochure when I was down stairs and there is this little cottage inn on the outskirts of town that serves traditional breakfast fit for a king. Most vacationers go there when they are in town. The clerk informed me the place is pretty popular."

"I'm ready when you are because I'm famished as well."

The inn was called Enchanted because it resembled the Enchanted Forest with its variety of plant life and water streams infested with gold fish. The inn had a sun deck located near a cave with a fortress that surrounded the place. It also had a large quadrangular court for any wayfaring person whose taste buds were about to water.

Nicole and her mother were led up a stairway to the upper level, a garden to be exact overlooking the beach. The place was so beautiful that it almost made people forget they were hungry. People were literally mesmerized by the inn's beauty. The beauty of the place was somewhat of a disadvantage because people were slow to order because they were always looking.

"Mother isn't this place beautiful."

"I've never seen anything like it in my life time" her mother said.

"The place looks and smells great," said Nicole.

The waiter took their order and as usual, they both ordered a healthy breakfast because they both were concerned about their calorie intake. Both were health conscience people concerned about heart disease, which is the number one killer in America. Nicole's mother was definitely trying to lower her cholesterol. She went walking three times a week. She always ate foods that were low in saturated fat since the death of Nicole's father who suffered from heart disease.

"Mother let's hurry up and eat because I would like to take some pictures of this place."

"I know what you mean because you would do this place an injustice just telling people about it. If you tell anyone that you actually visit a place like this, people would honestly think you were making it up. A person would actually have to have proof in order to say they have dined at a place like this. I definitely would like to show off the pictures to the ladies at my bridge club when I return home. They will be so jealous."

As they were finished eating Nicole's mother noticed this gentleman staring at Nicole.

"Nicole don't look, but it's this gentleman over there at the other table that has been staring at you since the time we took our seats. He's kind of cute."

"Mother there you go again; he probably is mesmerized by the beauty of this place like everyone else."

"Sure he is, your beauty."

"Mother if you keep this up I will stop taking you places with me. You are trying to get back at me for teasing you this morning about Mr. Smooth." Nicole said in a joking voice.

"No I'm serious, this gentleman is actually staring at you."

"Maybe I should stare back", said Nicole."

"No don't do that, that's rude, anyway he just walked out the door", said her mother.

As they went outside, they took plenty of pictures and walked on the beach. Nicole would have been satisfied just lodging on the beach but she had promised her mother she would take her sightseeing.

It was off to the Charleston Museum, recognized as one of the country's oldest museums. The museum was decorated with American and Colonial art celebrating the state's history. The museum also had a planetarium the tour guide informed them of the museum history which was founded in 1773.

Next, stop the Charleston Harbor. Nicole was intrigued with Fort Sumter, a place where the Civil War began. Nicole always has been fascinated with the Civil War because her father always told her stories about the war while she was sitting on his lap. He informed her that they had relatives that fought in the Civil War. Nicole felt that this was the main reason she did so well in history when she was in school. Nicole felt if she had not majored in business she would have majored in history and became an historian, a professor at a top University, teaching kids about history and how history is doomed to repeat itself.

Fort Moultrie, South Carolina, which is also located in the harbor, was a place that pays tribute to the brave colonist who fought against the British during the Revolutionary War. They also visited Fort Johnson and Windmill Point. The Charleston Harbor was a place with rich American History and there is no better place in America to find out about the images and impressions our forefathers made in shaping America.

Nicole and her mother were impressed with the history and artifacts because they felt if you do not know your history how can you progress in the future. Both were amazed how South Carolina just had a mixture of history and being blessed by Mother Nature. The next stop was the gardens. If South Carolina is known for anything, it is known for its beautiful gardens. They continued to take pictures; Nicole had purchased plenty of film.

The Middleton Place Gardens, which is the oldest landscape in the country, looked like the Garden of Eden because everything was already prepared and beautifully placed. A mixture of assorted azaleas and camellias filled the air along with ancient oak trees. Nicole's mother felt the gardens had more of a spiritual connotation then a natural one because it is a place her soul can rest in peace.

"Mother isn't this place peaceful. It almost seems it's in a world by itself."

"Nicole in my life time I have seen some beautiful places, but nothing can touch this."

Cypress Gardens was just as beautiful with its assortment of colorful flowers and several lagoons flanked by cypress trees. Magnolia Gardens had the distinction of being the most beautiful garden on the face of the earth some thought. It portrayed many different cultures. The gardens in Charleston presented a touch of elegance and were so moving that even Nicole, the cool and collected one, had goose bumps running down her spine.

The next morning it was off to Hilton Head where Nicole once had taken part in a leadership management seminar with the rich and famous. On the way to Hilton Head, they stopped off in Beaufort, South Carolina, a place also known for its beautiful gardens and historic mansions.

At Hilton Head, Nicole jogged along the coast. Hilton Head was so beautiful this time of the year. Robert use to visit the place with his golf friends each year to play in tournaments. They played here every year. Even though they talked about coming here for one of their anniversaries, they never got the chance. Robert use to rant and rave how beautiful Hilton Head really is. Nicole was somewhat reluctant to come because she knew Robert would take in some golf and she did not want to share him with anyone. Nicole was familiar with Hilton Head because she took part in a three-day event called 3-R, (Resolution, Rest and Relaxation). It was a seminar for people to actually network and talk about how America can pull together to make it a better place from the rich and famous point of view. The President attended the seminar one year. Nicole spoke at the seminar on gender equity relations in management among peers. Organizers of the seminar were very pleased Nicole had taken an active role. The seminar was a meeting of the minds that could not have taken place at a better location than Hilton Head, South Carolina.

Nicole and her mother had visited all of South Carolina's historical sites and had a wonderful time. Her mother fell in love with South Carolina because of its serenity and majestic natural beauty. She felt it was a perfect getaway from the city that never sleeps.

"Mom, I love you", Nicole said with tears in her eyes.

CHAPTER
5

Nicole arrived in her office precisely at five a.m. Her secretary had not arrived yet, and she wanted to get a head start in catching up on her paperwork. There was a lot of catching up to do since she had been to Martha's Vineyard and touring South Carolina with her mother. Everyone at Maywell was gracious enough to make her transition a smooth one upon her return from her sabbatical trip. She started out on the right foot by getting to know the employees there as well knowing the very make-up of the company. She had made several recommendations to the board as she came in with a very detail oriented business plan.

As she was sipping on some carrot juice while shifting through some papers she was very anxious to know what the board felt about her plan. Nicole had a vision for Maywell, but that's nothing knew now a day because everyone who seems to be in charge this day age says at one time or another they have a vision for this, or a vision for that. Hell, even our President when he took office stated he had a vision for America. Nicole felt some people were getting a little tired of people saying they have a vision for this, a vision for that. Not that, visions are out dated, the bottom line is people want results. How can you put money in my pocket in order to secure my family financially? That's the big sixty-four-thousand-dollar question. Nicole felt there was no job stability nowadays with all the layoffs and mergers that's frequently taken place in today's economy. These companies are making money, but fail to make as much money as they projected because they assume too much debt while the employees are made to suffer the consequences. Companies now are inflating their books, standard accounting practices. Nicole was aware of this and wanted to make every attempt to make Maywell profitable in the future by building up a reserve during the company's lean years. She knew people were counting on her to turn the company's aspects around. She knew people only believe what they see and all eyes were on her.

By no means was Nicole planning on becoming Maywell's savior, she wanted the workplace to be a relaxed environment with an open door policy where employees can feel at ease doing a job they loved and getting paid a hefty salary in return. Nicole knew a happy employee is a productive one. No hard line approaches here like her predecessor enacted his way or the highway. Nicole was just grateful that an opportunity such as this had come along, being the CEO of a company such as Maywell. Her only objective was to work for a progressive company such as Maywell with the opportunity for advancement. Opportunities like this come along once in a lifetime. It was seven a.m. and people were starting to arrive at the office.

"Good morning Nicole", said one of the secretaries who identified herself as Shelly.

"Good morning", said Nicole.

"Coffee, Oops! I forgot you do not drink coffee as she remembered Nicole only drank carrot juice and water in the morning, how about some carrot juice?"

"No thanks, I already have some."

The members of the board started filing in as they were led to the conference room.

"Good morning Nicole," they all said as they walked pass Nicole.

Nicole was scribbling some notes on a legal pad.

"Nicole, how was the time spent with your mother?" asked Mr. Aslong.

"Fine; how nice of you to ask John."

The meeting was called to order.

"Gentleman, I sincerely hope each one of you had the opportunity to review the business plan I drew up in order to secure our profits and move the company into the next millennium. It will enable us to continue to be the number one computer company in the world."

Mr. Dannerman looked in amazement, listening carefully, but in the back of his mind thinking Nicole was a cocky and arrogant bitch. Not realizing people felt the same way about him, that he was a cocky arrogant bastard.

"Granted the fact we will make some mistakes along the way, but hopefully they won't be detrimental and we can learn from them and move on. I will assign our most experienced reps with the least experience ones. Training programs will be setup to train these people. The IT program will be setup throughout Europe. The IT program will be designed to get people certified. I have targeted the universities in each major European city to teach courses and offered scholarships along with having seminars and updates in order to train small businesses throughout Europe so they can use our computers and software. We want to train the students in Europe, so they can get certified if they want to go into business for themselves or seek employment with Maywell we will have valuable candidates to choose from and they can promote our products. The biggest challenges in Europe will be getting through the red tape and our competitors."

Nicole had the board strict attention.

"I will name someone to head the European operations which will be in direct contact will headquarters via satellite through our computer network.

"Certainly," said John Aslong.

Kudos', they all yelled in favor of Nicole's plan. Nicole had just scored her first major victory as CEO.

Nicole looked at some notes she had scribbled on her legal pad before the meeting.

"I would like to reiterate that our European venture is our top priority. We will set-up a period in which we will monitor our operation versus the European economy so we don't spend wasted time and money in unnecessary acquisitions. We will review our course of actions directed by our research department to determine the parameters we should take. I want this operation up and running as soon as possible."

Ty Dannerman was sitting back recording or observing all the information like a sponge. This was valuable information that could be used against Maywell if he played his cards right. Timing would be everything and if he could score this coup with Conquest he had Maywell right where he wanted them. All he could see were dollar signs, but the true satisfaction will come when Maywell is utterly destroyed. Moreover, like Maywell destroyed his character.

Nicole named Aaron Sharpener to head Maywell's European operation. Mr. Sharpener had been with Maywell since he was eighteen. He started as an intern, but was passed over when it came to promotions mainly because he did not get involved in office politics. He knew his job and he knew it well. Nicole looked over his file and felt it was time Mr. Sharpener got his just due. She knew about the bad blood that existed between Aaron and Ty. Mr. Dannerman did not necessarily care for Mr. Sharpener; he was considered a computer and a financial wizard by his peers. Their personalities clashed along with their business priorities for the company. When Mr. Dannerman wanted to spend more money on mainframe computers rather than PC's, Mr. Sharpener indicated that Maywell's mainframe computers needed to take a backseat. Mr. Dannerman in turn insulted Mr. Sharpener intelligence by totally dismissing the idea. Mr. Sharpener called Mr. Dannerman a hypocrite and informed him that he was out of touch with reality. Mr. Sharpener strongly felt that PC's would be the rave of the future simply because they are more accessible. Mr. Sharpener was Mr. Dannerman's worst critic, which eventually would lead to Mr. Dannerman being ousted as CEO. It was the straw that broke the camel's back.

Mr. Sharpener was highly recommended by some department heads. Some of them sang his praises as he was the link that kept them together during the company's lean years. Ty deeply despised Aaron because they came from different backgrounds and felt Aaron did not have to work for a living, that he had not paid his dues. When Ty was CEO at Maywell he once went to Aaron's office ranting and raving about some financial records. Aaron was no softy by any stretch of the imagination kicked Ty out of his office and delivered those records to Mr. Dannerman's office wrapped in a chain. The message was loud and clear; this is not Egypt so don't ever crack your whip around here because I will not be intimidated. In another incident, when Mr. Dannerman wanted to cut cost through layoffs Mr. Sharpener marched right into his office again with a trash can filled with shredded paper and emptied it on Mr. Dannerman desk to point out, shredded paper means to shred jobs. Mr. Sharpener was his own man. Aaron came from an upscale family. Ty came from a modest family to say the least. They basically were hired together at Maywell. While Aaron relied on his skills, Ty relied on office politics to move up the corporate ladder while discrediting Aaron every time Aaron was up for a promotion. Ty felt Aaron was the golden child and had everything handed to him on a silver platter while he pulled himself up by his own bootstraps. Aaron drove the fancy cars when he was in college and as an intern while Ty basically had to work himself through college just for the bare necessities in life, like food.

Aaron had a wife and four kids, strictly a family man. He had a compassion for computers. He knew computers like the backside of his hand. He could make a computer do whatever he wanted it to. Nicole knew this and felt that Aaron was the right person for the job, it was a no brainer as far as she was concerned. Aaron had the business savvy and the wits to head the European operation. Nicole knew Aaron had plenty of opportunities to leave Maywell but he stayed. This showed loyalty even though some co-workers and his spouse encouraged him to leave because they strongly felt he was treated unfairly. The funny thing about Aaron was he always felt he would get his just do at Maywell one day. He informed his co-workers that "every dog has his day" and that a person may give out, but never give up. He felt he had put too much time and effort at the company and he did not want to just pick up and leave. He always wanted to work for one company and eventually retire there. He was waiting patiently on his pension.

Aaron's new position at Maywell was to carry Maywell into the next millennium as the number one computer company in the world, a financial prophet who would oversee a billion-dollar budget. When Maywell's cost rose over company projections Mr. Sharpener cut inventory cost without laying off people which was a stroke of genius. He spoke at seminars and had written several books on dealing with computers. He knew there would always be cost demons in the corporate world but felt a person would have to be creative in order to find a way of getting around it. He had an unorthodox style, which rubbed Mr. Dannerman the wrong way, but he got the job done. Dannerman tried vigorously to get rid of him but failed. He knew for certain that Aaron had concrete evidence that he had dipped his pen in company ink. The board would not go for that because the man produced results and that was the bottom line. Some board members knew that Dannerman wanted to put one of his cronies in that position anyway so they quickly shot down that resolution.

Nicole and Aaron went out for lunch to discuss in details what is expected of him. Moreover, it was just a get to know you lunch. Nicole wanted to make sure that Aaron knew he had her full support. The Hyatt Cafe was located in the business district of

Orangeburg. Nicole wanted to get away from the office on neutral turf plus the cafe had great food.

"Aaron I wanted to have this lunch just to clear the air".

"I understand perfectly Nicole. I know you made a judgment call by naming me to head-up the operations in England and I sincerely appreciate it," said Aaron.

"No Aaron I'm not here to judge you by any stretch of the imagination. I picked you simply because you are the right person for the job. I certainly know about the bad blood that existed between you and Ty. I feel it's inappropriate for me to comment on that particular subject; as far as I'm concerned that's water under the bridge."

"That's nice to know, but I must say what went on between Ty and my self was nothing personal on my part, just business. Everything I did was for the good of the company."

"Aaron I know that and that's the main reason I chose you. You are a team player, a true professional in every since of the word," said Nicole.

"Nicole I've heard a lot of good things about you and I truly feel you are the right person to lead Maywell into the next millennium. I know you have the board's full support."

"Thank you Aaron, now enough of the small talk, let's eat."

Nicole stayed away from asking questions about Aaron's personal life because that is off limits unless Aaron volunteered that information. As far as she was concerned, she knew all she needed to know about Aaron. Nicole always refrained from office politics. People in the office want to know about your personal life to draw you in so you can be a part of the so-called in crowd. It's like you're damned if you do and damned if you don't talk about your personal life in some shape, form or fashion. If you don't let others in on your personal life they will just speculate and perceive you to be a loner or stranger and if you do talk the information you tell them can be used against you later on down the road. That's one of the main reasons Nicole didn't go out to happy hours with people in the office. Loose lips sink ships and if it wasn't office related she refrained from attending. She knew Aaron had worked his ass off for the good of the company. He is a workaholic. He reminded her of herself. He is the first one to arrive at the office and usually the last one to leave. The joke around the office was that Aaron arrived before the custodians. He occasionally comes to work over the weekends in casual clothes to prepare for the following week. Even though he's considered to be a workaholic he found time to spend time with his family. He attends all of his kid's sporting events, helps them with their homework, and even takes them on family outings like camping. This was the type of person Nicole was looking for, a dedicated person.

Nicole had informed him that the offices in England had been chosen and it was necessary that he moved immediately. Aaron's family was ecstatic about moving to England. His wife spent several summers in England as an exchange student when they were in college. Maywell would pick-up the tab for a year or until they found permanent housing. Aaron was ready to go, for this would be the first major venture for Maywell and he was very happy to be a part of it all. Nicole informed him to give the Queen hell as they both had a big laugh.

The culture in England was very diverse and this was a welcome challenge. Aaron felt people should be judged by their character and not by the color of their skin. His main responsibility in Europe would be to create a diverse front for Maywell that represented many different cultures of the universe because we all are one if you want to believe it or not. He knew he would be spending many countless hours researching the foreign market. This suited him just find because for the first time he could just concentrate on the task at hand and not have to look over his back. He knew he had Nicole's support and he was going to make the best of it because you only have one shot to make a good impression.

·········

Nicole awakened at four a.m. went on her three-mile daily jog. Jogging became a ritual with her since her father's death, to raise money to find a cure for heart disease and diabetes. Several years after her father's death, she got involved in a race to raise money for research to find a cure for the number one plague that kills so many Americans each year. Even though she does not participate in the race each year because of her busy schedule she donates her time and money for this worthy cause.

As she arrived for work, early as usual she immediately picked-up where she left off the previous day. Today would be a busy day. She had an appointment to meet with representatives from one of the nation's largest marketing firms, Barnston & Co, a company that specializes in creating corporate designs to enhance a company's image. This job could have easily been handled in-house, but Nicole wanted outside influences to take on the task, something that has an international appeal, but with a personal touch. These designs would be put on Maywell's web site to inform the public of Maywell's ventures.

Nicole felt that Barnston & Co. could enhance the company's image especially with Maywell's venture abroad. Nicole knew that Barnston & Co. several years ago turned down the opportunity to work for Conquest due to creative differences. Conquest called Barnston & Co. a shallow marketing firm with soap-opera solutions. Barnston & Co. chooses their clients carefully, a company doesn't choose Barnston & Co., Barnston chooses you. They were good and they knew it, no bragging just a fact. They didn't have to advertise their services. They were internationally renowned and have work with some of the world's largest fortune 500 companies. They would prefer to work with start-up companies or floundering companies, companies that could really use their services. These companies usually rise like a phoenix; in turn Barnston & Co. gets all the credit, which in turn makes them a wanted company. Working with Maywell would be different, a chance to work with a company with a woman at the helm. This would be a win, win situation.

Maywell would pay a hefty price by calling on Barnston & Co., but Nicole had the support of the board so the price wouldn't be a problem. Maywell pockets were deep and the board had increased its marketing and advertising budget to launch Maywell's venture into England. Barnston & Co. consultants would interview Maywell's employees to find out their needs. They in turn will do a research study and make recommendations of the data they collected to the board.

The European operations would have a separate budget of its own; money had been allocated for that purpose. Nicole felt that a hefty advertising budget would increase sales in England and raise Maywell's market share on the NYSE. The market had been very unpredictable recently. The bear and the bull were fighting it out on Wall Street. Nicole, being the analytical person she studied the market on a daily basis whereas Mr. Dannerman when he was CEO relied on his expertise, trying to out smart the market. Maywell's shares fell downward because he misjudged the manufacturing and inventory aspects of the operation. He simply didn't look at the overall picture. Nicole was a strategist, her philosophy was to cut cost and carefully monitor Maywell's expenses.

Nicole had done her own homework on Barnston & Co. She knew the firm had three billion in billings and half of those billings were abroad. Barnston & Co understood the European market. They also had worked in China, and Japan.

As Nicole was sifting through her reports, Angela one of the office secretaries brought her some water. She asked Nicole was there anything she could get her. Nicole politely said no as she was biting gently into an apple.

"What's with all the files do you need any help arranging them" asked Angela.

"Not at the present time, but thanks anyway. I have them somewhat organized."

Nicole immediately turned her attention to the PC report. The file contained valuable information that Maywell will introduce in the coming weeks. Some of that information would be eventually stored on Maywell's web site. Maywell would be introducing a more accessible PC that would be less intimidating and highly affordable for the average user, a PC that can store more information on its hard drive. The screen looks more like a mirror than the average computer monitor with e-mail capabilities, which can be connected to a cell phone to check your voice messages as well as having a fax modem.

Nicole knew this was the information age and people have computers at home and use them more than they use their telephones. Computers have become such an integral part of society. Instead of people asking what is your phone number nowadays, they ask for your e-mail address. Maywell wanted to become the innovator in this information age before the market becomes to saturated. By launching these new computers Maywell could increase their revenue into the stratosphere. Maywell had to change the customer's perception about home computers by letting people know how computers have changed their lives and that they are now affordable, unlike years past. Maywell had spent countless hours researching how the public uses computers to prepare for the launch of their new computers on the market.

Just as Nicole was putting down the PC report, Angela buzzed her and said that James was there to see her. Nicole told her to send him in. James Savoy, the director of marketing at Maywell had been at Maywell for years. He knew all there was to know about advertising.

"Nicole, have you had the opportunity to look at the PC report."

"James, believe it or not I just finished looking at it."

"Good, we have several days to put the finishing touches on it before we formally introduce it on the market. All systems are ready to go."

"I sincerely hope so because we are about thirty days behind schedule. It was supposed to be on the market when Ty was CEO. Has something been left out that I'm not aware of?" asked Nicole.

"No, everything is in place until it can be updated. We just want to make sure you are abreast on everything because we want your input on this project. You pretty much know the rest as far as the revenues we are projecting for the upcoming fiscal year. Other than that everything is self-explanatory. Marketing has spent countless hours doing the research and working on last minute details on this project and we are expecting a warm response once people realize how they can benefit from having a home computer." said James.

"James, it seems to me you all have dotted all of your "I" s and crossed all of your "T's. I appreciate the time and the effort your department has put into this project. I commend you for that."

James had a profound respect for Nicole because she worked her ass off, unlike Ty. James perception of CEO's was that they simply don't work, that the word work and CEO don't belong in the same sentence. CEO's have these cushy jobs and sit around on their Asses all day and dictate and make rare appearances to the public. They just stock pile their money and gracefully retire rich and not giving a damn about their employees who make-up the company.

Ty Dannerman had left the office about noon and drove to Cross, South Carolina on Lake Moultrie where he met one of Art McRand's henchmen known only as Mr. X. Mr. X got out of the car, he knew it was Ty because he had phoned Ty from his car phone and Ty told him where to meet him. Mr. X noticed Mr. Dannerman's car, the man looked this way and that way and saw no one. The area was secluded. To be secret was his diplomacy.

"Good afternoon Sir. No one followed you here did they?" said the man.

"No dam it, I should be asking you the same question. Has the money been transferred to my Swiss account?" said Ty.

"Hush, not so fast, I need my information first before I reveal that to you." said Mr. X.

"Tell Art I don't like to deal with any of his cronies. The less people involved the less complicated things will be," said Ty.

"I don't know anything about nothing sir. I'm just doing my job. Anyway McRand is a high profile man, the less seen of him the better."

"Like I'm not, who in the hell do you think I am, a piece of chopped liver?"

"Sir, do you have any info for me or not. Patience is not one of my strongest virtues."

"Now who's in a hurry? Don't be so anxious. Maywell has hired Barnston & Co. to enhance its European operations and will launch its home computer project in the upcoming weeks, which is a nice gadget with e-mail capabilities and fax modems, the whole nine yards. Art might want to hurry up and beat those bastards to the punch to steal their thunder."

"That's all you have?"

"No, tell Art I've bugged Nicole's system and I will keep him informed, got it."

"Artie is looking at the big picture and wants you to collect as much information as possible in order to build a strong case to totally destroy them. Oh, by the way the money has been transferred to your Swiss bank account," said Mr. X

Ty was happy that the money had been transferred to his account even though he wasn't pleased or felt comfortable in dealing with Art's cronies. He opened his trunk and gave Mr. X a black box. Mr. X inspected the contents inside, like he actually knew what he was looking at. In the box were over five hundred Maywell Electronic microprocessors, computer chips that are the brains behind the majority of the personal computers, which Maywell will launch in the coming weeks. Enough info to make old man Maywell turn over in his grave.

Mr. McRand wanted the computer chips because it contained some of Maywell's top secrets in their computer bank. This would allow him to keep ahead of the competition. A few years ago the rumor mill had Conquest's going bankrupt, shares of the computer giant plunged forty percent at one point to an all time low that rattled Wall Street. Conquest vigorously denied the rumor. Even though he didn't come out and publicly and say, Mr. McRand blamed Maywell for Conquest recent troubles. Wall Street analysts were skeptical that Conquest could rebound and rise from the ashes. McRand informed investors that Conquest would battle back and overcome their financial woes. He indicated that bankruptcy was too strong of a word and that he had a plan to turn the company around. Conquest was simply in a make over phase and made broad product cuts. Their products weren't nearly durable as they once were. One mistake was they focused on quantity rather than quality, concentrating more on style than substance. Mr. McRand informed investors Conquest had made progress. The investors main concerns were would progress come fast enough to make a significant difference. They were confident for the most part because they had seen some progress. Conquest had improved customer relations due the help of a consulting firm they hired. Conquest needed to address their problems instead of passing the buck. This would enhance their image and make them more, customer friendly. Conquest rank second behind Maywell in the computer industry with about fifty billion in revenue. Conquest has always played second fiddle to Maywell, but during their lean years they lost some ground due to lost market share to Maywell. They lost nearly three billion in the third quarter in the previous year. Their stock is among the most widely held throughout the USA, once again second only to Maywell. Stocks have taken a beating on Wall Street recently so Conquest investors understood. Maywell stocks were down from its yearly high gains. Conquest investors were optimistic because the company recently started receiving quarterly profits after going public, shedding billions in debts, and establishing new credit lines.

Even though Conquest capital is not as tight as it once was, it needed something extraordinary to overtake Maywell as the number one computer company. Conquest board members scoffed at a plan to loan money to its customers to buy their computers. McRand wanted to target college students to extend them a line of credit on a payment plan with the bulk of the interest to accrue six months after they graduate. Board members didn't want to set aside a cushion to cover their losses. Conquest was still reeling from bad investments they made from other companies they invested in that took a serious beating. Their investments and loan portfolio had grown tremendously in the past year.

On the way back to Orangeburg, Mr. Dannerman lit a cigarette while listening to the radio. He had no regrets sticking it to Maywell; his conscience was seared by a hot iron. There was no turning back now, now that his plan is in full motion. Life would be grand, once he leaves the country when his deed is over. Back at the office he listens to Nicole's and James' conversation about Maywell's new PC that will be introduced on the market. He started listening to the entire conversation. He had bugged Nicole office and e-mail system. He had to monitor her every move if wanted to pull this off successfully. "You don't let someone take what you once had," he said to himself. "You don't get mad, you get even."

CHAPTER 6

On the day of the presentation in which Maywell would introduce its new line of PC's, Nicole's secretary was scrambling to get some information Nicole needed immediately. Her secretary was jotting down some last minute notes in shorthand as Nicole spoke to her. Nicole had requested the day before that everyone involved should arrive to work early on the day of the presentation. All those that were involved with the presentation were gathered in Nicole's office and it was quiet as a mouse, so quiet you could hear a pin drop on a piece of cotton.

"Is everything in place?" asked Nicole.

"We're all set to go." said her secretary.

The press conference was set for nine o'clock. James Savoy would be the one making the presentation, although this was expected of the CEO. Nicole insisted that Mr. Savoy do it, since he and his staff had done most of the work. Nicole wanted the spotlight on the product, not on her. She wanted to make James the front man so the public could realize that Maywell is a united organization in spite of its recent change of leadership.

At the press conference, James wore a blue, single-breasted suit with a heavy white starched French cuff shirt with the initials J.S. on the sleeves. Nicole wore a blue suit with a white handkerchief stuffed in the pocket along with a white blouse and panty hose with blue high heel shoes.

"Good morning," said James as he greeted the press.

"Today is a very special day at Maywell and for our customers. Our brand new PC can save you time and money. You will be able to send information much faster and more efficiently. He informed the audience of the computer benefits and features and how they would be able to analyze and process their data.

After the press conference, Maywell had a reception and handed out product information on their new PC. The corporate limo dropped off top executives of the company at headquarters to assess today's activities with some of Maywell's top shareholders.

Shareholders had a lot to celebrate because Maywell's stock rose three percent on the NYSE. It was a new beginning so to speak as one could picture old man Maywell smiling from the grave as he was reaching for his pockets.

Maywell could now turn its attention to operation Europe. This is what Ty was counting on because this operation could pay big dividends. With all the money that Maywell pumped into this venture they couldn't afford to make any mistakes. Maywell could lose the shirts off their backs. Any mistakes would be a costly one. Maywell had come a long way and this venture would be the ultimate challenge for the company.

Ty's secretary buzzed him.

"Ty, Nicole would like to see you in her office."

Ty was scrolling through some of Nicole's personal documents.

"What does she want?" he shouted.

Ty was pushing for time as he was planning on meeting Mr. X. He rushed to her office as he almost ripped his coat as he taking it off the rack. Nicole was sitting at her desk with a note pad in her hand with some of Maywell top executives in her office.

"Gentleman, Angela will bring in some refreshments for anyone who wants any. I want all of us to be on the same page concerning our new ventures and proposals that we will be dealing with in the near future.

One of the proposals Nicole was referring to was Maywell's joint venture with Moltra Telecom that would give Maywell customers more accessibility to their software programs. The project had already won broad approval from Maywell's Board of Directors and throughout the industry. Ty had tried to make this venture possible when he was CEO, but Moltra indicted that the timing wasn't right. Ty felt that Moltra had an ulterior motive, as they backed away from the deal. This venture would allow Maywell customers to use software applications for entertainment and business purposes.

Another proposal was that Maywell planned a joint venture with Kincade, Inc. to develop a series of product lines for their PC's, which included desktop and laptop computers. Kincade was an American company that developed powerful PC chips. Maywell wanted to do business with an American company since the Japanese had nearly cornered the market in PC sales. Maywell also wanted to send a strong message to buy American while attempting to scale back imports. Nicole wanted Maywell to round up more American partners as Maywell ventured into England. This would take away some of the financial burden as Kincade would market and promote the chip.

Nicole wanted Maywell to think like the customer. She knew everyone would like to own a computer, but the drawback was cost. So when the economy was at an all time low, Maywell kept up sales by cutting prices by offering customer rebates up to several hundred dollars per purchase. Nicole's idea was for the consumer to be able to think as little as possible when it came to purchasing a computer, getting the right product to the customer on time while providing outstanding customer service.

Ty sat back in his chair as visions of revenge danced in his head. He removed his reading glasses and cleaned them with his tie, just a show of interest as he jotted down some notes. The proposals Nicole introduced for Maywell were excellent ones, which provided specific details. The details provided communication, product knowledge, organization, and customer service structuring plans. Ty give Nicole her kudos', which was music to his ears. All he had to do was sit back for the ride. "Hell, this is easy" he thought to himself.

He looked at Nicole during the meeting in lust, seducing her with his eyes and wondered how someone so beautiful could have so much intelligence, wit, and charm. All the pretty women he ever came in contact with did not have anything between their ears. Nicole dressed to impress. She was a picture of beauty.

"We can pull this off", shouted one of the executives as the meeting adjourned.

"Yes", said Mr. Savoy, if we play as a team."

Nicole was on a mission and had the numbers to prove it. One of Nicole's main attributes in being a visionary was that she knew when to negotiate. She believed in confidentiality. She thought when she spoke. She was very analytical and weighed every option. Her computer was her bible. She kept confidential information on her computer to better analyze her thoughts.

She would be flying to London to meet Aaron as Maywell had installed a help line for customers to ask questions concerning any of Maywell's products. It was Aaron idea to install a help line to better inform the people of England of the products Maywell had to offer.

Nicole was looking over files Aaron had prepared and gave him kudos for a job well done so far when she e-mailed him. She didn't want any mishaps that could lead to any troubles whatsoever. Her motto was taking the time to do the job right the first time in order to save time and money. This venture would be an uphill battle especially with the economy almost at a stand still, if Maywell played their cards right they could still thrive during the economy slowdown. A company had to be creative and Nicole knew if anyone could pull this off Aaron could.

Nicole packed her bags, went on a jog before dinner. She was famished and hadn't eaten anything all day. This wasn't healthy, but it comes with the territory, which was not highlighted in her job description. She knew she had to maintain her health because she was always on the go. She took an assortment of vitamins in order to maintain proper health. She could hear her mother's voice in her head telling her she shouldn't be skipping any meals because no one can depend on their health. She maintained proper health by visiting the spa once a month to purify her body of poisonous toxins.

She thought she heard the phone ring, but it hadn't. She wanted to sit down and have a nice relaxing dinner and afterwards catch up on her riding. But as fate would have it the phone did ring and on the other end was Andrea. Andrea and Nicole were best friends, but hadn't talked to one another in a while.

"You know you are in trouble don't you," said Andrea.

"I know my name is mud and before you say anything else I have no excuse. I'm guilty as charged," said Nicole.

"We haven't talked in so long I almost don't recognize your voice."

"Andrea mother told me you asked about me and believe it or not I was really planning on calling you."

"You mean you actually had the time to talk with a love one."

"Andrea believe me, if I told you how busy I have been you would probably think I was lying."

"So don't tell me. I know Nicole; you are off the hook this time. Your mother told me she came to visit you. She said she enjoyed herself tremendously."

"Yeah, mother and I have a wonderful relationship and we did have a good time. I hated to see her go."

"Nicole we are all so proud of you."

"Thank you Andrea its nice to hear, coming from my dearest friend. Robert thought a lot of you."

"Speaking of Robert, your mother told me you found out some information concerning Robert's death."

"Well sort of, I told mother not to mention it to anyone because I'm not quite sure what to make of it. Let alone what my intentions are at this time."

"Whatever you decide I'm sure it will be the right thing to do. You have our blessings.

"Enough about me, mother told me you were pregnant again, this time with twins."

"What can I say my husband can't keep his hands off me," said Andrea.

They both had a big laugh.

"Andrea you have heard of this thing called the pill."

"Nicole, trust me the store is closed after this. I'm having my tubes tied when this is over."

Andrea and her husband, James had been married for twenty-three years. Her and Nicole married the men of their dreams, talk about a picture perfect romance. They use to double date all the time. Talk about their dreams of one day of having a big family. Neither men wanted their spouse to work, but it was their choice. It would have suited them just find if their wives had stayed at home and had kids. Robert and James were old fashion, but romantics.

"So when is the big day." said Nicole.

"In three weeks and I will be so glad Nicole, this have been a difficult pregnancy, my ankles swelling and my blood pressure always high."

"That's normal, plus you are carrying twins," said Nicole.

"I'm as big as a house. My elbows have turned inside out. But James has been very patient with me."

"He ought to be he is mainly responsible."

"You got that right. He makes sure I follow the doctor's orders by eating right and making sure I stay off my feet."

"That's great Andrea because there is nothing more important than prenatal care because what you do now can affect those babies for the rest of their life."

"James has been spectacular even though I have been a bitch at times."

"You have that right, especially carrying twins. Andrea you are blessed; James is one in a million. Some men are not sensitive to a woman's needs especially when they become pregnant. They go around parading cigars and have this chip on their shoulders like they are the ones having the baby. Some have the nerve to think their job is done after they impregnate us."

"Nicole I couldn't agree with you more. If James had been insensitive to my needs its no way I would have had three previous kids by him. The store would have been closed years ago. You know we both married men from the old school. They make a way out of no way. As soon as we ask it was done, no complaints whatsoever. They spoiled us in a way. It's no way in hell I could put up with some of crap the women of today put up with in their relationships, it's unheard of."

"James is a hell of a provider," said Nicole.

"So was Robert, Nicole. I know how much you wanted to become a mother."

"Robert and I always use to talk about having kids, but it just wasn't meant to be. We tried several years before he was called to Vietnam, but it just didn't happen."

"Well everything happens for a reason even though we might not quite understand. If you want, you can have some of my kids."

They both laugh. The doctors had informed Nicole and Robert they didn't see any reasons that they couldn't have children. Nicole and Robert didn't stress out about not having kids. They understood perfectly things happen in due time. When Robert was instructed to go to Vietnam they chance were cut short.

"Andrea we need to get together soon. I have to send you a gift, but I don't know what to give you. Do you know what gender the kids will be?

"No child, whatever, as long as they are healthy, we want to be surprised this time around."

"I promise you when I get back from London we will get together just like old times. We can exhale together. We definitely will need a break by then," said Nicole.

"You got that right. Nicole, take it easy and don't work your self to death. Take a little time out and smell the roses," Andrea.

"Tell James I said hello and keep his hands off you until you get your tubes tide," said Nicole.

"Easier said then done, Nicole," said Andrea.

"Goodnight", said Nicole.

"Bye Nicole and you have a safe trip," said Andrea.

Nicole finished eating and had time to catch up on her reading. It was late and she was tired.

CHAPTER

7

Nicole knew this would be a long weekend; there weren't enough hours in the day to do the things that needed to get done. She had a million and one things to do before her trip to England. This job was more than she bargained for, but she loved it. No time for a private life it seems. She thought about her conversation with Andrea informing her to take time out and smell the roses. A statement that is easier said than done. She remembered how life was so simple when Robert was living. They use to make time for one another. Now it's all work and no play and no one to share it with.

She prepped herself on the Moltra and Kincade files along with the information Aaron had sent to her. "There is only marginal room for error for mega deals like this," she said to herself as visions of old man Maywell danced in her head. She could literally hear him say "don't mess up." It was though he was breathing down her neck. There were over two hundred detailed pages of information stipulated in the contract that could mean billions for both parties. Maywell's finance department had spent many countless hours making the necessary revisions with the contract in which both parties would be satisfied with. Nicole had the final approval along with the board's support.

Nicole, looking at the long term wanted Maywell to get involved with the information highway because those who don't come on board now and pave the way will be at a serious disadvantage in Y2K. She wanted Maywell to create a world wired vision, computer networks set up around the globe to have the world at your fingertips. This could be pulled off if Maywell focused on its strengths in maintaining good customer service and the retail sales of their computers. Customer service was the key, Nicole had set-up deals with national restaurant chains to provide scholarships for kids, a Maywell computer with free web service for a year and whereas the kids that received scholarship money for college would be able to eat free at these national chains. In turn these national chains would be contracted in using Maywell's products. This venture was called "The Food for Thought Program." Nicole thought this was an interesting concept since the nation is struggling with its free lunch programs and recent reports on how unhealthy our youths are today which could lead to serious health problems for them in their later years. Nicole knew that money was tight for some college kids to pay for their meals. This would take a huge financial burden off the parents especially since some of these parents have been struggling, all their lives, some working two jobs, mortgaging their homes trying to save enough money to make sure their children get an opportunity to go to college. She had heard horror stories about some college kids going to bed hungry. Her heart went out to these kids because they could not concentrate on their academics if they are hungry. These kids are our future she thought to herself as she was looking over the contacts along with some other important documents.

She said "the hell with this," as she threw down the reports, the conversation with Andrea kept ringing in her head. It was such a beautiful day and she wanted to do some things she wanted to do for a change. She felt that the weekends, especially Saturday's should be spent sleeping in with rollers in your hair wearing pajamas, your robe with your house shoes on. She looked out the window and it was such a nice day, she decided she needed to get out and smell the roses. She went to the racquet club to play some tennis. She swam a few laps in the pool and afterwards went to the salon for a massage, manicure, pedicure, and got her hair done. Her motto is that, if you look good you feel good.

She started to feel guilty because there was work to be done and the pressure was there. She arrived at the office around two o'clock, wearing fresh tennis attire. There were no dress codes on the weekends. She looked over some more documents concerning the Moltra and Kincade deals. She could have used some help, but it was

Saturday and no one was around. She wouldn't dare ask any of her secretaries to come to work on Saturday's unless they volunteered because unlike her they have a social life and families they have to take care of, most of the people who usually work on Saturday's worked till noon. Only a skeleton crew usually worked on Saturday's in order to catch up on their work from the previous workweek.

It seems she had read every word in the documents a thousand times, enough to have them memorized. She marched down the hall to make some copies. This was a first, no one roaming the hallowed halls of Maywell. She had heard others employees say that they could still feel the presence of old man Maywell, but she actually didn't understand what they meant until now. As she was working down the hallway, pressure mounting, she actually felt old man Maywell presence for the first time. It was scary, unlike a ghost, but more like to an affectation, having confidence in herself to pull off a deal like this. It was like he gave her his stamp of approval, but at the same time saying don't blow it. She felt like she was between a rock and a hard place, damned if she did and damned if she didn't. It was like she was in a vacuum, old man Maywell's presence everywhere at home and at the office. Hallucinations were not part of her job description, but she soon realized it came with the territory with this damn job. Old man Maywell still had a strong hold on the company and will smother the holy hell out of you if didn't get the job done. He was intimidating as hell, an SOB in every since of the word, but he got results. Nicole had read old man Maywell's biography in Maywell's library and knew he didn't tolerate hardly any mistakes. He didn't want you to do the best job you could possibly do, but he simply wanted you to do your job. Employees at Maywell had a small window for error if you wanted to work for old man Maywell. The money was good, but there was the stress factor that came along with the job. If you couldn't take the heat you had to get out of the kitchen or as old man Maywell put it "get the hell away from around him" because he would dismiss you like a bad habit.

·········

The Concord landed precisely at ten a.m. at Gatwick Airport London time. It was a beautiful spring like day, kind of surprising for London especially since it is known for its misty weather conditions. There was a like fog that covered the horizon, but all and all the weather was beautiful. Nicole was met and greeted by Aaron who hugged and gently kissed her on the cheek. It was a kind gesture to say thank you Nicole for having faith in me. In the company's limousine they caught up on their pleasantries, for it had been a while since they last saw one another.

They had become phone pals and sent one another a million e-mail messages, faxes; they had teleconferences during their separation. Nicole felt the information highway had its disadvantages. The main reason was that it's so impersonal. You cannot give someone a handshake after a business deal or transaction. Aaron had grown a beard and Nicole found it hard to picture Aaron with a beard since he was always clean-shaven when he was in the States. But Nicole didn't have a problem with it since it wasn't stated in Maywell's dress code policy. The policy only stated that you be neatly groomed. Nicole was lenient concerning this matter because she trusted her employees to do the right thing.

Nicole wanted to jump right in with the business aspects of Maywell's operations in England. Aaron insisted that she relax and recuperate from the jet lag and would fill her in on all the details concerning what's been going on in England because there would be a series of grueling meetings that would require a lot of time and energy on their part. Aaron suggested he was in no hurry and suggested to Nicole to take a day or two off to relax or do some sightseeing. The thought had crossed Nicole's mind because she wanted to visit some of England's historical landmarks. She had been working fifteen hour days and felt she needed a break. But every time she said this there was always some work to do.

The limo dropped he off at her hotel. Aaron told her his wife had prepared dinner for her and that the limo would be back at seven o'clock to pick her up. Nicole unpacked, showered and had the time to take a nap. Even though the Concord got her to England in record time, Nicole was tired nevertheless from all the grueling hours she had spent getting this project off the ground.

At Aaron's house Nicole was amazed how Aaron's kids had grown. She figured time actually doesn't wait for no one. Aaron informed Nicole that no Maywell business would be discussed over dinner tonight. He wanted her to sit back and relax while enjoying a home cooked meal. He knew the countless hours Nicole had be working. Aaron's wife and Nicole exchanged pleasantries and started talking fashions as dinner was about to be served. It had been a long time since Nicole had actually sit down and had a home cooked meal. She could cook but she was tired of eating her own cooking, not to mention eating alone. She had a sign in her kitchen that read, this kitchen is closed due to illness, *I'm sick of cooking*. It was nice to sit back in a family atmosphere and enjoy someone else's home cooking for a change. As dinner was served Nicole couldn't help to think about, this is what she and Robert had visioned, sitting down and having dinner with their kids. She got all choked up. Everything was so nice and dinner was fit for a king as Aaron's wife had prepared all of Nicole favorite dishes. After dinner they sat and talked about old times and world affairs. It was getting late and Aaron took Nicole back to the hotel and informed her to go sightseeing tomorrow and they would get right into business later on in the week.

The Tower of London located near the River Thames was on a roughly hewn lodge estate in the heart of London. The ninety-foot white tower was occasionally visible as a light fog around formed a dense cloud with a scenic view.

A dialogue of discomfort filled the air as symmetrical star-shaped stone chambers with wooden doors were home for political prisoners. As Nicole walked through the chambers with other tourists she could fill a chill, emphatically rushed down her spine. For a brief moment she could feel the pain and agony of what Thumps More felt. For over a year, More was a political prisoner, confined by the carefully carved stone walls in the Tower, refusing to acknowledge King Henry VIII as head of the church in England before he was executed.

Nicole began to understand why the pilgrims landed on Plymouth Rock in order to avoid execution and to worship as they please.

As Nicole was walking through the chambers she stopped and read some of the dialogue inscribed on the walls. The twelve-acre estate is still called home by some yeoman's and their families. Her only source of light was candles burning on a chandelier hanging from the ceiling in a cold, damp dreary cell. It was so cold she could have worn a coat. But within the dark hallowed walls she could capture a sense of being from her studies in European history in college. As she read from her history books she would always try to picture in her mind the essence of what she was reading. Reading from her textbooks was a lesson she would never forget because reading is a wonderful experience. She strongly supported Ophrah's book club because it encouraged people to read.

As the tour guide was explaining how the lower part of the Tower represented Shakespearean history, Nicole was in awe as she was admiring the original structure of the Tower built in 1078. The tour guide also explained how William the Conqueror made the Tower a fortress while leaving no stones unturned.

Nicole met a yeoman couple that had lived at the Tower some forty years. They explained to her how that they felt a sense of security since moving there. They also explained to her that they felt institutionalized, part of history. While dining at the Tower Thistle Hotel, Nicole stared at the Tower Bridge where sunset painted the skyway red. As she gazed up at the sky she remembered reading in a news article how the galaxies portrayed a stick like figure of a red man.

Nicole learned from the couple how that England's culture is like no other. Women in England were the breadwinners in the household while the men stayed at home. The men stayed at home and to do the chores, they are widely known as beefeaters. The men were the one's who sat around and gossiped at the local pub, talking about their families and old military stories over a game of cards and checkers. As Nicole was sipping on a cup of tea, the couple went on to say that the men in England were comfortable with the women being the breadwinners. The men were not inferior to the women; they were content with being at home. Society has made tremendous strides, but for the most part women are still considered to be inferior to men especially in the business world.

Nicole could definitely identify with the women in England because of her position at Maywell. The income of women in England is basically controlled London's financial district. One of Maywell's market research reports done before they ventured into England indicated that women in England use computers for business purposes while the men used computers for recreational purposes like playing computers games and downloading music. At any rate that's why Nicole wanted to venture into England because the market was in high demand for computer technology. Job growth in England was at its all time high. Computers will be in high demand and would bridge the gap between high tech jobs and the information highway.

This would be no easy task because the structure of the English government is heavily bureaucratic. Once known as a conservative party, the word change is an obsolete word that relates to the English Parliament. Having outside corporations coming in is like invading in unfamiliar waters. During those lean years, England's economy suffered as unemployment soared and wages and benefits plummeted. There was no union to protect the employees. Most corporations stay away from places where the economy is unstable, but not Maywell, the innovator and trendsetter of this millennium and the millenniums to come. Old man Maywell created a cash cow.

During England's reconstruction period, Nicole wanted to jump on the bandwagon. Her strategy was one of precise decision-making. Her plan was making companies in England change the way it does business, something that would jump-start the economy. She knew she would need help from the English Parliament in order to breakdown bureaucratic barriers and formed a legal team to work with Aaron. The government would purchase computers from Maywell in order to start new businesses. Maywell would provide the technical know how that would train employees and would eventually set-up scholarships for anyone that wanted to major in the technical field while training new and existing workers.

Analyst thought this was a brilliant idea, but risky. They knew if anyone could pull this off Maywell could simply because they had the resources. Analyst knew Nicole had the expertise with her international experience, but the big question that remains was timing, timing was everything.

Nicole's vision was to get the people to think technical before the next millennium because that's where the projected job growth will be. She felt that there would be thousands of jobs in the technical field by Y2K, but not enough people to fill them, not that computers will take the place of people because computers cannot fix themselves. Nicole felt there would be a shortage of certified technicians by Y2K. She understood that more technical people were needed to expand the workforce in order to have a world wide vision.

Nicole visited the home of Princess Diana, one of the most elegant private eighteenth century mansions in London. The mansions in London are beautiful with a lot of history behind them. Nicole admired the magnificent paintings and sculptures that hung on the hallowed walls of the Spencer House. The house was a creative dialect that would put anyone in awe of its mastery. The mansion is located behind a Green Park on a densely wooded and perfectly manicured estate in the heart of London.

Nicole took snapshots of the mansion's beautiful interior designs. She was so mesmerized and thought for a moment she was in a fantasy. She had read about the neo-classical architecture in school while she was studying European history. The brochures didn't do the mansion any justice because the mansion had recently been renovated to capture its cultivating decor. The mansion was full of antiques, art works, and sculptures like the essence of the eighteenth century.

Nicole's next stop on her tour was Whitby, known as the city of Count Dracula. Nicole thought that this Yorkshire town was very intriguing because it was a diamond in the rough. Whitby stands on the mouth of the River Eske like Egypt stood on the Nile River. It kind of reminded Nicole of Egypt especially after the ten devastating plagues because Whitby looks like it sits on a sepulcher. The churches in Whitby look like they are consumed. Whitby reminded Nicole of the event in the bible on how the stones in Canaan Land were heaped in rubbish and were consumed with fire upon the children of Israel's return from Babylon.

Nicole found Whitby to be a mixture of different cultures. The ancient remains from a historical view that would take your breath away and the fishing ports, which reminded her of Charleston, South Carolina. Both cities have pubs along the bay area that attracts a lot of tourist. Like Charleston, Whitby was famous for its monuments, which pays tribute to their hero's. Charleston has Fort Sumter, the site of the opening battle of the Civil War. Fort Johnson was the place where Americans seized tax stamps from the British in opposition of the Stamp Act. Whitby pays homage to Captain James Cook who sailed the South Seas along Whitby coastlines.

Nicole admired the museum that honored the late explorer's life from everything, which would include mementos, painting, and the ships he navigated. Nicole enjoyed the atmosphere in Whitby. It was a wholesome atmosphere, which seems to escapes the troubles of the world, a friendly place where people walk their dogs along the seaside.

Nicole also enjoyed the North York Moors Nahona Park. The park reminded her of Middleton Place Gardens in Charleston which has this certain mystic about it. Robin Hood Bay, a romantic hideaway was similar to Martha's Vineyard. This was a place Robert would have loved she thought to herself, just being one with nature. People were picnicking on the grounds, which had an assortment of beautiful flowers.

Nicole hopped on a train to gaze the countryside. She saw an old stone farmhouse in the Moors while sheep were gazing the fields. Nicole saw more animals on the road than automobiles, which she thought was very unusual. It was getting late as the fog was beginning to settle in, putting a yoke around Whitby's neck.

The train came to a squeaky halt and Nicole got off and walked the puddled alleyways and the crooked cobblestone streets looking for a cab to take her back to the hotel. The foghorn had sounded as darkness fell on Transylvania. The cab stopped, picked up Nicole and faded into the sunset.

CHAPTER 8

Operation Europe was ahead of schedule, thanks largely to countless hours Aaron had strung together since coming to England. He brought Nicole up to speed on what had transpired in the past several months. Conference calls, e-mail messages, and faxes are one thing; both Nicole and Aaron preferred the hands on approach. Nicole had to be brought up to speed on over two hundred pages of documents, in which every "I" was dotted and every "T" was crossed. Aaron had personally researched and drafted all of the documents.

Aaron never complained about the countless hours he spent heading the operation. He thrived on the pressure. It was his family that suffered the most, but the situation was tolerable because they knew how important this job was to Aaron. Maywell had assembled a dream team to work with Aaron, some of the top legal and corporate minds money could buy.

It was Monday and Nicole, Aaron and members of his dream team was to meet with the English Parliament and some of England's top dignitaries. Aaron spoke in a candid and distinguished manner. He expressed the importance of the operation while giving a detailed report of Maywell's objective and aims of the operation in compliance with the bylaws of the English government. He also informed them of how both parties could benefit from this operation by setting up a computerized network system throughout England. He handed out product information on how Maywell products will help in the development of small businesses.

One of the products Aaron was talking about was Sparcomat, an automated system for all companies in England in order to increase their production. Aaron indicated that start-up companies would be the focal point that would jump start the economy and major corporations would soon follow. Sparcomat would allow businesses to store and send information efficiently, which would enable a business to produce documents electronically which would save time and money. Sparcomat would allow Maywell to monitor customer performance by providing outstanding customer service and helping them get the maximum benefit out of their businesses.

Sparcomat had been in development for several years. Retest after retest, Sparcomat was placed under scrutiny by some of the powers to be at Maywell, mainly by the man himself, Ty Dannerman, creative differences was the stumbling block that kept Sparcomat grounded. The ongoing feud between Ty and Aaron made it almost impossible for Maywell to progress into the next millennium. Ty was jealous that Aaron would get all the credit for this project and there was no way in hell that was going to happen. Aaron had developed a software package only to be shot down by Ty and some members of the board. Constant in house bickering nearly destroyed the company.

All and all, Nicole was impressed with all the time and effort Aaron had put into the project. She wasn't surprised because she knew Aaron was the right man for the job and he would be rewarded dearly.

"Aaron, you have a done a magnificent job why don't you take some time off and spend it with your family, I know they would appreciate it," said Nicole.

"Thank you Nicole, but I'd rather stay around here and keep a close eye on things."

"Aaron, I'm sure things won't come crashing down if you take some time off. That's what your staff is for."

"Yes I know, my family does feel a little neglected, but they will manage. They know how important this project is to me."

"But family is more important. When I was at your home for dinner the other night Julia kind of let on how little time you spend with her and the kids these days. I know this project has consumed you and I do not want your wife to think I am a slave driver and working you to death."

"No Julia knows that you are not running a dictatorship. In due time, I will take some time off, but not now."

"Aaron I can't emphasize enough, how much I appreciate the job you have done in such a short period of time. It's simply amazing, I know Rome wasn't built in a day, but you give the people who built it a run for their money."

"Nicole since you have taken over I have more time to be creative in order to do my job. It's more like a sense of freedom."

As they were in Aaron's office chatting, one of Aaron's secretaries delivered an urgent message, which informed Nicole that she needed to call headquarters immediately. Nicole knew it was late in Orangeburg and figured it was due to some type of major crises. Another secretary come running down the hall almost out of breath into Aaron's office and informed Nicole someone was trying to send her a sky fax in Aaron's office. The fax was sent by no other than John Aslong, which informed Nicole to call him immediately. Now Nicole was really worried, but tried to remain calm. But as she was phoning Mr. Aslong her heart was in her mouth wondering what in the world could be so important.

"John I got your message. What's wrong?" Nicole said almost out of breath.

"Nicole we have a major problem; you need to catch the next flight back to the States."

"I figured it must be a major problem brewing, but does it require my immediate attention. I want to wrap things up here before I head back to the States," said Nicole.

"Yes it does require your immediate attention. I am sure Aaron is on top of everything over there. We need you here because of those deals we had with Moltra and Kincade, Inc."

Nicole didn't let him finish she cut him off in mid sentence, so abruptly.

"John what are you talking about, those deals we had. Those deals per say were suppose to be signed, sealed and delivered."

"Well Nicole as I was getting ready to say. Those bastards reneged on our official offer."

"They did what!!!" Nicole shouted through the phone.

"They backed out of our deal, but that's not the bad part. The bad part is they signed with those SOB's at Conquest."

"John tell me you are kidding because I know its not April Fool's Day." said Nicole.

"Nicole I wish I could, but I'm not joking. Those bastards signed with Conquest."

"But how, it was supposed to be confidential until all the paperwork was signed and only then we were to go public about the venture. How did Conquest know or anyone else for that matter know we were in negotiation with them?"

"Nicole that's the mystery, we don't have a clue." said John.

"This is hard to believe," said Nicole.

"Believe it, how they found out is beside the point, especially right now. It could have been anyone who worked for the companies that leaked the information, granted the fact that mega deals of this magnitude are hard to keep secret for long," said John.

"Unbelievable." said Nicole.

"We just have to suck up our losses. I'm not that concerned that we loss the deals. This type of thing happens all the time in corporate America. I'm just sick in my stomach we lost out to Conquest of all people," said John.

"John I will catch the next flight out."

Nicole had a sick feeling in the pit of her stomach. Aaron shouted to one of his secretaries to bring Nicole a glass of water because she had turned pale. Her worst fears finally had become a reality, losing out to your archrival. Visions of old man Maywell danced in her head. She felt she had let him down, even though she had no control over what transpired, Nicole always took things personal, she hated losing.

"Nicole what happen?" said Aaron.

"John informed me that those deals with Moltra and Kincade, Inc fell through."

"You got to be kidding."

"I wish, but the real kicker is that they signed with Conquest of all people."

"Come on, you got to be kidding me."

"You heard me, Conquest."

"Damn, this is crap. Something sounds fishy," said Aaron.

"That's water under the bridge now."

"Can't they be sued for breach of contract, or something." said Aaron.

"I wish, but no, we just have to deal with it. Plus, I hate coming across as a sore loser," said Nicole.

"John didn't give you an explanation of the specifics concerning the deals."

"No I guess I will find that out when I get back to headquarters."

"He didn't blame you did he?" said Aaron.

"No he didn't, I guess I should blame myself. Maybe I overlooked something."

"Don't go blaming yourself Nicole. This type of thing happens all the time. At least those bastards should release a statement on why they reneged on the deal."

"I guess I find that out when I get home", said Nicole.

"I would demand that those bastards give me one. That's the least they could do."

"Believe it or not, they owe us nothing, but we will see," said Nicole.

"Man, man, man, I'll tell you, Conquest of all people. I know they are basking in the glow of finally getting one up on Maywell. I guess that old saying is true, every dog has its day."

"Well Aaron if that's it, I'm going to head back to the hotel and pack and try to catch the next flight out."

"That's it for now. Nicole don't worry everything will be all right. If you need anything call me." said Aaron.

CHAPTER
9

It was a long trip home for Nicole in more ways than one. She was searching for answers on what went wrong and how to keep this thing from ever happening again. She knew John was right, that this type of thing happens from time to time. Stranger things can happen but this was highly unusual, not in a million years did she ever suspect that this kind of thing would ever happen to her. She thrived on being perfect and not ever having a blemish on her record, especially not now, a person in her position. What would her critics say? The nay Sayers that opposed her becoming CEO at Maywell, saying a woman can't do a man's job. "I told you so," would be the first thing that would come to their minds. Then a quiet voice told her to calm down, that she was making too much out of the situation. No one blamed her. She was putting the pressure on herself. She wanted to call her mother because she always made her feel better. She knew her mother would tell her to have confidence in herself. Never once did she doubt her abilities, after all John informed her she still had the board's full support. But damn, how did this happen? That was the question that kept ringing in her mind. "Think positive Nicole," she said to herself. You had a successful trip to England. Aaron has everything in order. Concentrate on the good things Nicole. You will pull through this. Look at it as a minor setback. Nothing more nothing less, people don't give you credit for the good things that happen so don't take credit for the bad either." That's what Robert use to always say. This voice was her guide, which kept echoing in her head.

There were a lot of chores to be done around the house. Doing them would help keep her mind off the problems at work. She was gone for several weeks, but it seemed longer. She wondered where to start, indoors our out. It was such a lovely day maybe she should do some work in the flowerbed. Pulling up weeds or plant some new flowers. Maybe she should do some cleaning inside and open up the house and let some fresh air in. She decides to do both, she would start inside and work her way outside. That way she won't have time to think about work at all until in the morning when she faces members of the board.

It was getting late and she was tired. She ate, took a long hot bath and watched a little TV. She played some soft music while reading The Wall Street Journal. There was an article on the front page talking about the deals that Conquest had pulled off. A big picture of Art McRand smiling like a rat stealing some cheese would about sum it up. She couldn't bring herself to read the article. She put down the paper and picked up a Forbes magazine, same article and same picture. She threw it down, "enough is enough already" she said to herself. She saw that Conquest stocks had rose somewhat on the NYSE since the deals with Moltra and Kincade, Inc. Conquest stocks usually are dormant, but recently had seen a little activity the past quarter. This was because they too had changed the way they do business. Her mind wondered back on the Moltra and Kincade deals. She couldn't take it anymore. She had to find a way to get over it somehow or lose her mind. Nicole did not want the board to see her sweat, nor bent out of shape. All she could think about was old man Maywell pointing his finger in her face just like the old man on the army poster, saying "Uncle Sam Wants You."

This was the lowest she had ever felt since Robert's death. Then all of a sudden it seemed like she could feel Robert's presence as though he was reaching out to her. She could hear his voice speaking to her saying "there is no gain without failure. You have followed your dreams and aspirations while a lot of people talk about them. You have actually accomplished them. You don't take credit for the good things that happen nor should you take credit for the bad things either. Life goes on and a lot of people are counting on you. Those people are living their dreams through you. So don't let them down. Don't let me down. I love you, keep your head up."

"Oh Robert I love you so much," she said to herself as tears came rolling down her face.

Right then she knew everything was going to be all right. Even though Robert was gone it still seems he is looking out for her, her guardian angel. That's what drives her, accepting her responsibilities as a person and boldly walking into them. She turned out the lights, said her prayers, fell off to sleep. Tomorrow would be a brand new day.

As expected representatives from Moltra and Kincade, Incorporated released a statement stating why they called off the deal with Maywell and signed with Conquest instead. Philosophical differences were the reasons they gave and indicated Conquest was a better fit to get them where they wanted to be by Y2K and that Conquest provided them the best opportunity to be more creative. The statement also indicated that their change of heart was not personal, just business and by no means should it be conceived as a negative reflection on Maywell. "Oh please, give me a break, don't patronize me", Nicole thought to herself as she read the statement. She thought the statement was pure hogwash, an insult to her intelligence. In the meeting the board reassured Nicole that she had their full support and vowed to overcome this minor setback. "A bump in the road", one board member called it.

Meanwhile Conquest was rationing in the glow. They had a lavish party at the Omni Hotel in Atlanta to celebrate their newfound wealth while their stocks rose considerably on the NYSE, which made investors very happy. Broadway musicians and dancers entertained over five hundred guests. Caviar was served while champagne gushed from a fountain. Company executives received Rolex watches. Old Artie was the toast of the town as Forbes featured him on the cover of their magazine as top executive of the month for pulling off a coup of this magnitude.

Needless to say Mr. Dannerman was very happy and benefited greatly from Conquest's new-found fortunes. He was tickled to death as he sat back with an unlit cigar in his mouth leaning back in his chair with a copy of Forbes magazine in his hand with his partner in crime on the cover. "This is just the beginning, and revenge is so sweet", he thought to himself as he read the article. It was full steam ahead, he had to go for the gusto and if anyone got in his way they would pay dearly and he does mean anyone.

CHAPTER 10

It was back to work as usually and losing the Moltra and Kincade deals to Conquest seemed like a distant memory. It was like a bee sting, it hurt at first, and then the pain soon subsides. The board informed investors that Maywell would rebound from this setback; a mere setback is what they called it. Deals come and go and there will be other companies that would want to do business with Maywell, for instance, the Ultra contract that happened to fall into Maywell's lap. Ultra was a communication giant in the entertainment industry that was looking to be a part of the information highway. When the deals with Moltra and Kincade fell through Nicole felt that joining forces with Ultra would create more of a global appeal for Maywell. The timing was right even though the slumping economy had many companies cutting back. For the third time in less then five months, interest rates were cut in order to jumpstart the economy.

What made this deal so sweet was, the company was basically owned by women. Since Nicole was hired by Maywell, the Census Bureau reported that companies owned by women had increased by thirty-three percent.

Ty didn't interfere with this deal because he didn't want to arouse any suspicion even, though he had reached deep into Maywell's computer banks, he needed to lay low. Plus, the deal was too messy. There were licensing agreements and copyright laws to deal with, things that only an insider would know and if Maywell lost out on this deal they would become highly suspicious.

Ty met Art in Goose Greek, South Carolina and explained to him about the Ultra deal and what their next move would be.

"Art my man you looked awesome on the cover of Forbes last month," said Ty.

"Yeah just like that Rolex watch on your wrist." said Art.

Ty was wearing the Rolex watch Art had given him when Conquest won out on the Moltra and Kincade deals, just a show of appreciation.

"Art I'm watching every move them SOB's make because I have direct access to the computer files at the company," said Ty.

"Did we bust those bastards bubble when we won out on those deals?"

"Art you should have been a fly on the wall. We got them where it hurt."

"They didn't get suspicious did they," said Art.

"Art believe me, they were too shock to be suspicious, and they don't have a clue to what went down. They are scratching their heads as well as their Asses. Those bastards were totally caught off guard, like a deer caught in headlights," said Ty.

"In other words they had their heads up their ass."

"That's putting it mildly," said Ty.

They both laughed. You could literally hear them laughing a mile away.

"Keep up the good work. We won this battle but the war isn't over. Watch your back and don't trust anyone," said Art.

"Funny you would mention the word trust Art because I would never have thought I would ever be in cahoots with you," said Ty.

"Get to the point Dannerman. I know you didn't call me way out here to criticize me," said Art.

"Be patient Artie, the deal with Ultra would allow me to use Maywell's software in various ways, to let me know what Maywell was bidding on, but not only that, but product information also. I got access to some of Maywell's top computer designs and you can beat them to the punch and eventually get a patent off those bastard's hard work," said Ty.

That was music to McRand's ears as he gazed up at the sky. He was thinking of his grandfather and how sweet revenge can be.

"Dannerman let's go for the juggler and bury those SOB's. Old man Maywell had a reputation for messing over people. Even though my grandfather wouldn't condone my methods in seeking revenge, he would be happy to know that Conquest finally overtook those bastards. This thing is too important to me; I want to literally destroy them bastards. Old man Maywell and my grandfather slugged it out for years. Grandfather tried to take the low road and reason with that SOB," said Art.

"Yeah, I heard stories about old man Maywell and how ruthless he was. In his autobiography in Maywell's library they picture him as a self-made man. How he pulled himself up by his own bootstraps and built the company from the ground up," said Ty.

"Self-made my ass, that SOB literally stole the company from under my grandfather's nose. He was definitely for himself. I just hope the bastard is rotting in hell," said Art.

"Old man Maywell was a high-roller looking for the big game and would destroy anyone that got in his way," said Ty.

"Yeah, he harassed grandpa for years and hunted him down like an animal." Old man Maywell was a damn slime ball, a disgrace to the human race and would do anything to make a dollar. Whether it was ethical or not, the bastard didn't have an ounce of integrity. Even though he wasn't formally charged, there was a federal probe that he gave kickbacks to political activist who were close allies to some top government officials in Washington to win government contracts. On the other hand, my grandfather was the salt of the earth, may his soul rest in peace. A religious man who cared about everyone, he would give you the shirt off his back, a man that would cut off his right arm before he would harm anyone. He was a family man and taught all of us to be self-sufficient," said Art.

Ty didn't particularly care for all the sentimental BS Art was telling him about his grandfather, even though he had a valid point. He wanted Art to remain focused on the business at hand and not get carried away with all the emotional crap. Nevertheless, he had to put up with it.

"Art my man, let's concentrate on the business at hand and remain focus," said Ty.

"I am focus, damn it. I'm more focus than I ever been in my life. I watch my grandfather die right before my eyes and it wasn't a damn thing I could do about it. Till this day, that shit hurts like hell. I vowed then I would get back at old man Maywell for killing my grandfather. Even though his ass is rioting in hell, I'm hurting that bastard where it hurts the most. I'm messing with his legacy. My grandfather wasn't afraid of that bastard; he was just too big of a person to pay attention to him. He was always turning the other cheek. But not me, old man Maywell left me with no choice but to go after his ass, even from his damn grave. If it were possible, after it's all said and done and my revenge is complete I would snatch his ass up from the grave and spit in the bastard's face. He was Satan personified in a body, Judas Iscariot revisited, kissing up to my grandfather one day and stealing from him the next."

"Damn Art that's deep. I can honestly say that old man Maywell's spirit is still alive and well running cold through the hearts and minds of the members of the board. I want to get back at those bastards as much as you do. They made me the laughing stock of the industry."

"Dannerman you cannot begin to understand my motives for wanting to get back at Maywell. It runs much deeper than your reasons. The difference between you and me is that you could have remained CEO at Maywell, but you burned too many bridges. You used your power for personal gain and if you are going to do that you have to be very subtle. You made your move to soon, you were to damn hasty. You bullied them. Patience is the key if you want to play this game. You were too radical for them. Hell, I wouldn't be surprised if those bastards weren't watching your every move, in and away from the office. They were looking for a reason to get rid of you, like a bad habit. You never want to give anyone a reason or ammunition to use against you. That can be fatal. That's why they replaced you with a woman. Someone that they felt they can connect with without having to look over their shoulders, someone more trusting, in other words someone that they can easily intimidate. Because if we get mad, talking about the male gender, we would tell you to kiss us where the sun doesn't shine, get my drift. I hope I haven't offended you in anyway, but I've been in this game for a long time and I know how it's played."

Ty listen attentively to Art, even though he didn't care to hear it, he knew Art was right. The truth hurts. He began to think about of his own beginnings. As Art was speaking he saw his own childhood flash before his eyes. How he overcame a bout with ADHD, a disease that attacks the central nervous system in children and had to take the drug Ritalin for most of his young life. He and his mother were never close because he blamed his mother for his condition. Even though there is no medical evidence, Ty's mother Alexis was very young when she gave birth to him and she was a party animal. Doctors had informed her she wouldn't be able to have children, which gave her all the more reason to party and not practice safe sex. She did not want to give up her lifestyle for the sake of her child. She continued to drink alcohol, smoke cigarettes, and take non-prescription drugs without the advice of her doctor during her pregnancy. Doctors had informed her she might want to consider having an abortion because there was a good chance the child could be born deformed. Alexis's family values wouldn't even consider her having an abortion and she wanted to have a child to love her to make up for the void in her life. Plus, she wanted to hang on to Ty's father, John; the old keep a man baby because he came from a well to do family.

Ty's grandmother Kim raised him along with his younger half-brother David who died at an early age from complications of pneumonia. Ty's father, John did take care of him financially and paid for his private schooling. If it hadn't been for John's financial support, Ty would have been a lost ball in high weeds because Kim didn't have the time of day for him after Alexis's death of an apparent heart attack at a young age. Kim tried vigorously to relive her youth and was putting Ty and David off on someone else to keep. Ty wanted desperately to live with his father who rarely visited him, but knew his wife wouldn't go for it. John already had a real family. Ty eventually felt his upbringings affected his marriage to his wife, Jane who recently filed for divorce. Ty felt the only reason she married him was for his money and when he was ousted as CEO she filed for divorce. Ty felt it was a status quo thing with Jane.

"Art that's where you are wrong, this thing is equally important to me as it is for you. My reasons may be more magnified. I will do whatever it takes to destroy those bastards at Maywell even if I have to…"

"Even if you have to what, what damn it," yelled Art.

"Art we are in this thing together; we are in way to deep to turn back now so don't go freaking out on me now."

"Ty don't go off the deep end, I want everyone to remain breathing, okay."

"Your grandfather didn't remain breathing did he? You said it yourself that old man Maywell killed him. The only difference is he didn't use a gun. Hell, death is death. By any means necessary will I make them pay? Art you are a so-called religious man don't the bible say do unto others as others have done unto you."

"You are a damn hypocrite Ty. You don't know a damn about the bible so don't go quoting shit. You don't know what the hell you are talking about. You need to proceed with caution and let the chips fall where they may."

CHAPTER
11

Flight 101 had just landed as Nicole waited anxiously at gate seven to greet and meet Andrea. It was a hot and humid day, but Nicole didn't mind the drive from Orangeburg to pick-up her childhood friend from the Columbia airport, after it was announced over the intercom that flight 101 was pulling into gate seven amidst a crowd of tourist. Nicole had a video camera to savor the moment because it had been along time since she last saw Andrea.

Andrea came forth amidst a crowd of people carrying her luggage. They both embraced one another. Nicole was astonished at how great her friend looked after just recently giving birth to twins, a boy and a girl named Robert and Nicole. Nicole couldn't wait to see the baby pictures, but first there was some catching up to do.

It had been four years and seven months since they last saw one another, too long to be exact, but who's counting. It seemed like this day would never come. Both of them had this day marked on their calendar, so it seemed. There were letters and phone calls during that time, but nothing can take the place of actually being together. They hung out a lot growing up; you didn't see one without the other. They were closer than Ophrah and Gayle. Andrea had just started her own consulting business after deciding not to have any more kids. Her top priority was having kids, but after Nicole was named CEO of Maywell she wanted to become a career woman as well.

"How is everyone," asked Nicole.

"Everyone is doing wonderful", said Andrea.

They loaded up the car and headed back to Orangeburg. They reminisce about old times on the way to Nicole's house. Aretha Franklin's song Respect was blasting from Nicole's speakers. That was their favorite song back in the day, two ambitious young women seeking respect. Andrea was surprised Nicole remembered, as the two was singing along with Aretha. Anyone that drove by would have thought they had lost their minds because they both were singing at the top of their voice.

Andrea fell in love with Nicole's house. The scenery wasn't bad either. Andrea was an easterner and thought the scenery in South Carolina was cultivating.

"Okay my friend, its time to exhale", said Andrea.

"Andrea we have plenty time for that, but first I've made dinner plans for the both of us and after that we can hang out, just like old times," said Nicole.

"Sounds like a plan to me," said Andrea.

"Take your time and unpack and freshen up and then we can go out and do the town," said Nicole.

"How's the job coming along Nicole," asked Andrea as she was getting dressed.

"Fine, I can't complain, it's everything I thought it would be and more, but just like everything else it has its ups and downs."

"Are the people at Maywell receptive to you? You know what I mean by you being a woman in charge," asked Andrea.

"The people there at Maywell have been wonderful to me so far especially most of the board members. Hopefully I won't step on anyone's toes."

"What do you mean most of the board members has been nice to you? Shouted Andrea, shouldn't all the board members have welcomed you with open arms?"

It seemed like Andrea wasn't going to let Nicole get a word in edge wise. As she was asking question after question before Nicole could get a word out of her mouth.

"Well I don't particularly like to judge people, but its kind of a unique situation. The gentleman I actually replaced still works for Maywell and he is on the board as well. He is kind of strange."

"You're right, it is a unique situation that he is still around. Why didn't they can his ass all together? He shouldn't be still lurking around; anyone knows that's bad business savvy."

"Well Maywell is a unique company and prides itself on its employees. They called it restructuring. To be perfectly honest they have never actually fired anyone in the history of the company, even though old man Maywell didn't tolerate mistakes. People retired wealthy and few quit," said Nicole.

"Restructuring my ass, the big question is, why would he want to stay there? If someone canned or replaced my ass I wouldn't want to continue working there," said Andrea.

"Well like I said, Maywell is a unique company. At Maywell the less questions you ask the better off you will be. That was old man Maywell's creed. He wanted all his employees to remain loyal and one would have to earn his trust. It was his way or the highway."

"But what don't you like about this guy? What's his name?

"Well to answer your last question, his name is Ty Dannerman. I just get a weird feeling when he is around. I guess it's a feeling of guilt. I kind of feel guilty because I replaced him. I'm sure that's all."

"Nicole you have always been a good judge of character and if that SOB does anything inappropriate you nail his ass to the wall," shouted Andrea.

Nicole was hoping that it wouldn't go that far because it's a messy situation when it comes to sexual harassment. She knew that sexual harassment and other complaints must go through the company mandate; the victim's peers and not a judge hear cases like these. The peers are usually paid-off by the company to protect the company reputation to dismiss so-called claims. Nicole felt it was just another way to discourage women that they are out of their league in corporate America.

They had a great time at dinner at the country club. They went to a jazzy nightclub to hear some jazz with the featured artist being none other than Bonny James. Even

Rick Braun showed up as a special guest. It was like they were still in college, but a little more sophisticated. The night was still young, but they wanted to hurry back to Nicole's house to catch up on old times. Back at Nicole's house they changed into something more comfortable. Andrea was still feeling the effects of jet lag. Nicole put on some soft music, took out bucket of rice cream because they both were on a health kick. Now it was time to exhale.

"What is a beautiful woman like you doing staying in a big empty house by her self," said Andrea.

"Andrea who said I'm staying by myself," Nicole said with a serious look on her face.

This was sure a Kodak moment because Andrea's mouth almost dropped to her knees as the rice cream she was eating dribbled everywhere.

"All right then let's hear it, out with it," said Andrea.

Nicole chuckled at Andrea who was waiting for the ball to drop.

"Andrea you know if I had a man in my life you would be the first to know. Plus, I'm to busy to have a personal life."

"Nicole you know how that old saying goes, all work and know play makes you a dull person."

"Well dull I must be because I simply don't have the time for a personal life. I'm not sure I want to be with anyone. The dating game has changed since we were in college. People are playing too many games nowadays," said Nicole.

"Nicole you have to make yourself available. I man isn't just going to fall out the sky."

"Funny you would mention that word because that's where my head has been lately, in the sky."

Andrea immediately knew Nicole was talking about Robert.

"Nicole I'm just kidding. To be perfectly honest I can't even picture you with any other man than Robert even though Robert is gone. In fact, I would be hurt to tell you the truth about it. I know it sounds crazy or even selfish because I still have the love of my life," said Andrea.

Even though the picture is unclear, Andrea credits herself for introducing Robert to Nicole. While Nicole said Andrea didn't have anything to do with it since they basically grew up together. They still disagree till this day. But one thing they both agree on, it was a match made in heaven and that true love only comes around once in a lifetime.

"Nicole, Robert and James are men that come along once in a lifetime. I knew you and Robert were meant to be because you both shared the same dreams."

"Yeah I knew we were the perfect couple. It was love at first sight," said Nicole.

Nicole hadn't been with any man since Robert's death not to mention no man had even come close to arousing her sexually. Robert was simply irresistible because he knew her worth. She loved his sophistication because he had an air about him that would make any woman week in their knees. Their sexual alliance was conformed to each gentle touch; the foreplay was gratifying. They found confidence through one another's eyes. For the eyes are the windows of one's soul, lovemaking at its finest that took them places neither had been before. It was like an outer body experience, the third heaven to be exact if one can explain it, or as the mighty O'Jays put it, climbing the stairway to heaven.

Andrea and Nicole talked to the wee hours of the morning and both fell asleep on the floor. The bucket of rice cream was empty and the music still softly playing. It was morning and they both woke up looking a mess according to their standards. It was to be a busy day doing woman stuff, but first Andrea had to check in on her kids. She called and spoke to James and the kids were okay as Nicole was yelling in the background at James. James just told them to have fun and that he missed Andrea.

This reunion worked out well, Andrea got the much-deserved break she needed from her kids and Nicole needed a friendly face to take her mind off the failed Moltra and Kincade deals. She had buried herself in her work so much so that she actually forgot what it felt like to have fun. Nicole's idea of fun was reading all the letters Robert sent her during their courtship. She kept those letters in a shoebox in her attic.

Money was certainly no object this day because they bought something at every shop between Orangeburg and Charleston. The next day they drove up the coastline to Myrtle Beach. They were trying to make up for all the years they missed seeing one another because they didn't know when they would be able spend this kind of time together again. They made the round trip across the state and now it was time for Andrea to depart. It had been a wonderful week, which neither would ever forget. As they were saying their goodbyes at the airport they both cried and vowed to see one another soon.

"Love yah Nicole and take care of yourself," Andrea shouted as she boarded the plane.

....

Sparcomat was proving to be a huge success in England, far above anyone's expectations. Nicole and the rest of Maywell's board were thrilled, as well as Mr. Dannerman who had reservations about the project at first.

During their weekly conference call, Aaron expressed his enthusiasm with Nicole. Who gave him his kudos' for the umpteenth time?

"Aaron never in my wildest dreams did I think Sparcomat would have this much success in such a short period of time." said Nicole.

"Our sales have nearly tripled, far above industry expectations," replied Aaron.

"Aaron our resource potential in England is untapped. The people in England have been very receptive and it's all do to your hard work Aaron. I knew you were the right person to get the job done," said Nicole.

"Well I have a great supporting cast; I can't take all the credit, but thanks anyway for having confidence in me. The training was the most important thing for Sparcomat. The training provided the basic foundation in getting people to understand the task at hand. And once the people here became comfortable in what we were trying to accomplish they were very receptive. The Universities here played a major role by offering courses and sponsoring seminars to help our cause, said Aaron.

Nicole changed the subject.

"Aaron how's the wife and the kids."

"They are doing great," said Aaron.

"Aaron you deserve to take some time off," said Nicole.

"Funny you should mention it. I will be taking some off and taking the family on a extended vacation throughout Europe."

"Good for you because it's well over due. Heaven knows you deserve it," said Nicole.

"Well my family has been very understanding: not to mention patient. I think it would be good for all of us just to getaway."

"Aaron you have my vote for father of the year. Anyone who can juggle a career and still be a devoted father has my vote and my hat goes off to you because you have not forgotten your first priority, think family first because life is too short," said Nicole.

There was a pause in their conversation as Aaron could detect a sigh in Nicole's voice. He immediately knew Nicole was thinking about Robert. His heart went out to her, but he knew it wasn't a damn thing he could do. The best thing he could do in this situation was to be quiet because he didn't want to say the wrong thing or worst tell her something he thought she should hear. The only thing he could think about was how could a beautiful woman, who has the world at her fingertips still be so sad. He felt she got a raw deal out of life, but we must play the cards we are dealt.

Now it was his time to change the subject.

"Nicole, I meant to ask you earlier. What was the reason Moltra and Kincade gave for signing with Conquest?"

"Aaron if you ask me it was a bunch of hogwash, but at the end they indicated it was philosophical differences that would prevent them from being creative. I figured Conquest must have sweetened their initial offer. I have no proof. One never know when you are dealing with Conquest," said Nicole.

"That's strange, how Conquest knew we had a deal on the table let alone the specifics of the offer," said Aaron.

"Aaron I asked myself that question a thousand times and just decided to let it be. This sort of things happens all the time and certainly it won't happen to us a gain.

"Well I guess you are right, some things in life we just don't have control of. But I assure you of one thing if Conquest was involved something shady went on," said Aaron.

"Aaron I was thinking along the lines, maybe they didn't want to do business with us because of me," said Nicole.

"Nah, its something else we just don't know about and I think we may be better off in the long run in not dealing with them shady bastards if they decided to change in mid-stream like that. That's not reputable," said Aaron.

"I guess we will never know the real truth so I just have to leave that alone plus I got bigger fish to fry. I'll be flying to D.C. on official business to get with some lobbyist on Capitol Hill and try to win some government contracts," said Nicole.

"That's great I know you will sway them with your charm," said Aaron.

"I'll do my best, but it will be a difficult task because the Department of Defense is cutting back on some of their operations. They have trimmed the budget tremendously since last year," said Nicole.

Nothing was closer to the truth because the Defense Department was closing some of its military bases around the country. Military personal wanted and deserved higher pay wages. Maywell shareholders and investors felt if anyone can pull this off Nicole could. They didn't want to doubt her, just look at what happen with Sparcomat. Nicole was lobbying for the Warsaw contract. This contract would allow Maywell to provide the government with all electronic devices including NASA.

Nicole boarded a plane to D.C. Government officials worked well with Nicole. This was because she had her feet already in the door by being friends with senator Gatewood. It was Nicole's job to convince the people on Capitol Hill that this could jump-start the economy and creates new jobs and update military bases around the country.

The flight landed at Dulles Airport and Nicole caught a taxi to the hotel. The traffic was horrible, for it was rush hour in D.C. as commuters tried vigorously to make their way home. D.C., a city of power which the world always has its eyes on, a city that transcends like no other. A city recently voted the number one place to be single in order to meet your mate, home of the movers and shakers of the world. D.C was like Nicole's second home. She visited the city at least once a year on Memorial Day to pay tribute to America's fallen heroes, how ironic she scheduled this trip during this time of the year because the entire top bureaucrats were there.

She always had mixed emotions about Memorial Day because the people who died in servicing their country only got recognition once a year. This was so sad because the people who lost their love ones miss them everyday. Nicole strongly felt something more should be done in honoring our fallen heroes. She would walk up to the wall and see Robert's name inscribed on it and it took every fiber of her being to fight back the tears. No one but the victim's family could ever imagine what she was going through.

Nicole befriended a woman at the wall whose husband died in the Vietnam War who the President will honor along with her at the ceremony. It took the government twenty years to positively identify, through DNA testing, the remains of her husband.

This woman had been waiting in limbo for years; finally, she can put some closure to all this madness. She didn't seem rancorous towards the government. During that time, she could only speculate on her husband fate, but at least now she has some peace of mind, unlike Nicole who is still struggling with the uncertainty surrounding Robert's death. Robert still remains an MIA, which leaves people like Nicole with lots of questions not to mention many sleepless nights. The word missing has a variety of meanings from prisoners of war, missing in action, or death. This is the type of situation that stirs up emotions in people like Nicole, a day late and a dollar short. The uncertainty was literally eating her alive.

The woman, who name was Kate, had bought several pictures of her late husband. Also the woman was accompanied by some of her late husband's friends giving testimonies on his behalf. Kate had literally traveled all around the world trying to get answers concerning her husband death, but had no success. Nicole felt the woman pains. Plus, she simply didn't have the time to go chasing around the globe on a wild goose chase like Kate. Nicole and the woman exchanged numbers and addresses in hoping to organize more groups to help the families of people who lost love ones in the war.

At the ceremony the President of the United States took center stage.

"Today we are gathered here to pay tribute to our fallen heroes who with courage fought for our country. Even though these people are not with us today, they are alive in our hearts. The memories that they've shared touched our lives so deeply, memories that we will always cherish. For those who lost their lives fighting for our country to protect the rights of all mankind, they are our role models. Their great deeds should inspire and encourage the living, not just on this day, but everyday. So let us not misinterpret this day with feast and gatherings. But let us remember and get the true meaning of Memorial Day which should be everyday in honoring our fallen heroes."

Everyone gave the President a standing ovation as he finished his speech and placed a reef along the great wall. Media personnel were rolling the cameras while photographers were taking snapshots to put on the six o'clock news.

Nicole walked over to the wall where Robert's name was inscribed. She could feel his presence as though he was near. Then there was a voice that called out her name, it startled her at first then she felt someone touch her back, it was senator Gatewood.

"Hi Nicole how are you doing?" asked the senator.

"Okay considering the circumstances," senator.

"Nicole I know I haven't been in touch with you recently as I promised when we were at Martha's Vineyard. I haven't forgotten about our conversation. I've been digging, but I really haven't found any concrete or encouraging information concerning the circumstances of Robert's death."

"I completely understand senator I know you got more pressing issues to deal with and its probably best to let sleeping dogs lie anyway. You are dealing with a smoking gun. I befriended a woman at the ceremony today who ran into all sorts of problems trying to get information concerning her husband's death only to find out twenty years later that he indeed was a victim of the war."

Senator Gatewood couldn't keep a straight face as he talked to Nicole because he was lying. The truth of the matter was that he had found some encouraging information concerning Robert's death. The information was sketchy at the time do to the conflict between the U.S. and North Korea concerning trade and weapon agreements. Plus, North Korea's recovery methods were very complex to say the least. The senator thought it was best to wait until he gathered some more concrete information before he actually told Nicole anything. He didn't want to get her hopes up. He promised Nicole he will stay on top of the situation until he found out something.

"Senator I know how close, you and Robert were, but the more I think about it the more discouraged I become. I just don't want to go through all that. Lobbying Congress on Capitol Hill to declassify records, it's simply not worth it. Sixty Minutes, 20/20, and Dateline have done documentaries on MIA's in the Vietnam War. How families have traveled across the globe that tried to get information on the remains of their love ones. I know that the U.S has sent search teams searching for remains of servicemen missing from the Vietnam War. Some of them have lost their own lives searching for the MIA's remains in Cambodia, Laos, Thailand, and Vietnam. I just don't have that kind of time. If I had one shred of evidence Robert was alive I would be on my knees crawling on the ground in Vietnam sniffing out clues like a watch dog looking for any clues I could find surrounding his death, just to put some closure to all this madness. I know Robert would like for me to keep looking forward and not look back. I have carried this burden around with me for years and it eats at you like a cancer. Although I'm not angry, but can't help from feeling I was robbed of the most precious thing in my life. Even though Robert loved his country and was willing to die for it, I really thought he felt he would make it back home. Dam it, Robert promised me he would and I believed him because he has never lied to me," said Nicole.

"But Nicole," said the senator who tried to get a word in edge wise.

"Senator I can't relive those events because the pain is too deep. I spent many sleepless nights because Robert's death still haunts the hell out of me. It took me a long time to finally accept his death and now you saying there may be some encouraging news surrounding his death. I can't deal with that right now. Do you understand senator?" said Nicole.

The senator knew he did the right thing in not revealing any information whatsoever to Nicole concerning Robert's death. He hated not saying anything, but he knew it was the right thing to do.

"Nicole I fully understand how you feel, but I still feel obligated to find out the truth and put some closure to all this. Robert was like my brother and the uncertainty concerning his death haunts me as well. It's also a burden I carry around with me everyday. Each time I look at this wall I can't help but to feel there is always hope that he may be alive, if not at least identify his remains. I definitely will keep in touch."

"Okay senator you do what you have to do and I will support your every effort," said Nicole.

"That's the way I like to hear you talk. Come on let's mingle, there's some people I would like you to meet," said the senator.

"Sure, whatever you say," said Nicole.

They walked along the wall and ran into some of the senator's fellow constituents. They exchanged pleasantries, shook hands and talked about world affairs. Some of the self same people the senator introduced Nicole to some of the very ones that could help her with the contract with the Pentagon.

They ran into Mark Thread, a senator from Austin, Texas. Mr. Thread, senator Gatewood, and Robert shared the same tents in Vietnam. They were as close as the Three Musketeers, they formed their own fraternity, and they were blood brothers.

"Mark this is Nicole Gershom, Robert's wife," said senator Gatewood.

"Well we finally meet, you are as beautiful as Robert claimed you were while we were in Nam. Robert that old devil, what a lucky guy, said senator Thread.

"Why thank you senator, what a nice thing to say, but I feel I'm the lucky one," said Nicole.

"Robert use to talk us to sleep talking about you," said senator Thread.

Robert was certainly a talker," said senator Gatewood.

"How is everything going at Maywell these days," said senator Thread.

"Everything is just peachy, said Nicole.

"I remember reading in the Wall Street Journal that you were named CEO of the company, finally a company had some guts to do the right thing," said senator Thread.

"Now if we can get a female in the White House we really would be up to speed," said Nicole.

They all laughed.

Both senators took Nicole by the hand as they walked along the wall. Nicole wanted to talk business while she had two of her biggest supporters by her side. Plus, she wanted to take her mind off the Memorial Day ceremony. The senators introduced her to the President of the United States.

"Hi Nicole it's nice to finally meet you, I'm one of your biggest supporters and I've heard you have done some wonderful things at Maywell," said the President.

Nicole was impressed; she knew the President prided himself in knowing everyone he comes in contact with. Why not, it's a great networking tool to collect money for his party. He made himself available to help his cause, his fellow man or his party. Nicole had read articles on how the President burned the midnight oil, staying up late, working the phones trying to garner enough support to push his policies through the house and senate. Nicole also knew the President was a master at persuading people to see things his way. What a valuable interpersonal skill to possess. He had the charm and the charisma to make himself equal to everyone.

"Senator Gatewood told me a lot of good things about you, as for Robert, he was a brave man and our country could use a few more men like him. People like Robert are our role models more so than I because they gave they lives for a worthy cause," said the President.

"Thank you Mr. President," said Nicole.

"Nicole, senator Gatewood informed me about the circumstances surrounding Robert's death and he has my full support. I've drawn up a bill that will make it easier for people like yourself to get a full account of MIA's and put some closure to all the madness. The bill will also include financial assistance for people who fought in the war and their families. I personally want Memorial Day to be everyday. Even though I didn't fight in the war because of medical reasons, my heart goes out to them and their families. I know I could never do enough to ease the pain of losing a love one under any circumstances, but the least I can do is to introduce legislation supporting MIA research," said the President.

Nicole was totally impressed with the President. It proves you can't judge a book by its cover. Nicole had read so many negative articles concerning the President. The President wasn't too favorable in the eyes of many Americans with scandal after scandal that rocked the White House, which Nicole felt some of those attacks on the President's character was unwarranted, instigated by special interest groups, all and all Nicole felt he was doing an effective job under the circumstances.

The President invited the senators and Nicole to be his guest for the evening at the White House. At the White House, Nicole met and greeted some members of the President's staff along with the first lady, who like Nicole was a strong woman; the first lady and Nicole had a lot in common. They talked about everything from fashion to a woman's place in politics and corporate America. They also talked about world affairs and how to make this country a better place to live, especially in the next millennium. Nicole got a few barbs in about business and the main reason she was in D.C., to persuade or influence officials at the Pentagon to form an alliance with Maywell Electronics. The President didn't want to seem bias on Nicole's behalf, but he wished her well and told her he believed things would work out in her favor. The President gave Nicole a proclamation on Robert's behalf for his bravery in Vietnam. Senator Gatewood was mainly responsible for this because he had informed the President on how Nicole was having a tough time coming to grips with Robert's death and at the same time trying to run a major conglomerate like Maywell.

As the evening was coming to a close, the President thanked Nicole and told her to keep up the good work. Senator Thread invited her to attend a fund-raiser for his re-election campaign in Austin, Texas next month. Nicole promised him she would definitely attend.

Nicole made her presentation at the Pentagon and everything went according to plan. Both parties agreed in principle with working with one another until the papers were signed. Nicole spoke with the headman at the Pentagon, none other then Mr. Bill Cordova. Nicole had heard he was a tough cookie, but fair. She felt if she could get his endorsement then Maywell would get the contract. Mr. Cordova was very impressed with Nicole's presentation, more so with her stunning beauty. He virtually couldn't take his eyes off her during her presentation. But that was nothing new; hell most men couldn't take their eyes off Nicole when she walked into a room or anywhere else for that matter.

Nicole left D.C. the next day on a flight back to Orangeburg feeling very confidant and why not. She attended the Memorial Day ceremony, made new friends, met the President of the United States, and strongly felt she had a deal with the Pentagon.

Back at the office, Nicole was going through the documents concerning the Warsaw contract with the Pentagon. Nicole wanted the contract signed, sealed, and delivered in the next several weeks. If she could have had her way the contracts would have been signed before she left D.C., but one of the drawbacks of working with the government was dealing with all the red tape and legal issues concerning contracts of this magnitude. Nicole knew these types of government contracts take time when you are dealing with a bureaucracy, but all and all it would be beneficial. She had looked at the numbers and by getting this contract would propel Maywell's profit share beyond the sun, moon, and stars.

CHAPTER 13

ustin, the state's capital, located in the heart of Texas was named after Stephen Fuller Austin, an American pioneer. The city resides on the terraced bluffs along a bend on the Colorado River. The city's architecture dominated the skyline. The city of Austin is known as the educational center of Texas.

Nicole was looking forward to this trip. She arrived a few days early in order to do some sightseeing. She had never been to Austin, just Dallas and Houston on business. She had heard a lot about Austin because Robert visited the city once and fell in love with it and wanted to move there. Austin is known for its recreational areas and artificial lakes surrounded by mountains and were recently nominated as one of the safest cities to live in America.

Nicole wanted to visit the Elizabeth Ney Museum, which resembled castles in England. Senator Thread had e-mailed Nicole an invitation to his fund-raiser with an attachment that read, "Everything is big in Texas," which Nicole thought was cute. The e-mail message also contained some sightseeing information on some of Austin's favorite attractions like the O. Harry Museum. Nicole couldn't wait to see some of these attractions, which senator Thread made out to be a paradise.

She was to have dinner with both senator Thread and senator Gatewood tomorrow evening at the governor's mansion. Senator Thread informed Nicole in the e-mail message that there would be a special guest present at the function, which would be held at the municipal auditorium.

Nicole's phone rang in her hotel room and it was senator Thread's wife, Sandra. She told Nicole she had some tickets to see Willie Nelson in concert, which starts at eight o'clock at the stadium where the University of Texas played their home football games. Nicole was an average music lover. She felt that it was only two types of music; either it was good or bad. She wanted to relax for tomorrow's festivities but decided what the hell and that it might be kind of fun; the concert was for a worthy cause. Plus, she had a brand new pair of blue jeans and cowgirl boots she wanted to break-in along with a cowgirl hat she just recently purchased.

The limo picked her up in front of the hotel. Sandra was waiting in the limo.

"Hi Nicole, its nice to finally meet you," said Sandra.

"The same here and thank you for inviting me to the concert," said Nicole.

Sandra was a country music fan. She was born and raised in Nashville, Tennessee, she practically grew-up at the Grand Ole Opry. She tried a stab at country music herself, but gave it up for medical school. She did some studio work by singing backup for some of country music biggest stars before she decided to give it up.

"Mark has told me so many nice things about you. I feel I already know you in some respect and I'm so glad you were able to make it to Austin," said Sandra.

"Believe me the pleasure is all mine. I was looking forward to this trip and anytime I can help out a friend of my late husband I'm glad to do it," said Nicole.

"We definitely could use your help. Is this your first visit to Austin, Nicole?" said Sandra.

"Yes it is. I've been to Dallas and Houston on many occasions for business purposes, but I haven't had the pleasure to visit Austin even though I have heard some nice things about it. My late husband, Robert use to rant and rave about how beautiful Austin is and I can see what he was talking about because what I've seen so far has been cultivating," said Nicole.

"Austin is a beautiful place, it kind of resembles home to me," said Sandra.

"Where is home", said Nicole.

"Nashville, Tennessee, the Grand Ole Opry," said Sandra proudly.

"Yeah, I see what you mean, you should feel right at home here," said Nicole.

"Mark brought me down here on spring break once to meet his family and I've been in love with Austin every since," said Sandra.

"I don't know much about Mark, only that he and Robert were good friends in Vietnam," said Nicole.

"Well, Mark was born and raised in Austin. He was involved in the ROTC in school before he joined the Air Force and got called to fight in the Vietnam War," said Sandra.

"How did you all meet? Austin and Nashville seems a world a part," said Nicole.

"Believe it or not we actually met at a football game. The University of Texas was playing Vanderbilt University and we met through mutual friends and stayed in touch with one another and the rest is history," said Sandra.

"Sandra I hope I didn't get to personal, but I'm a sucker for true love. I have so many fond memories of how Robert and I first met. It was true love at first sight it seems even though we were young and didn't even know the true meaning of love. But we knew we would always be together," said Nicole.

"By no means are you getting personal, I truly understand, I'm a sucker for true love also," said Sandra.

Sandra was all too proud to talk about how she and senator Thread first met, but she didn't want to get too carried away talking to Nicole about love since she lost her spouse in Vietnam and senator Thread survived the war.

"The Vietnam War affected so many people lives'," Nicole blurted.

"I know what you mean, Mark left for Vietnam after the second semester of his junior year. When Mark was sent off to Vietnam it was pure hell at first until he got to know Robert and senator Gatewood. They formed a fraternity in Vietnam. I think Mark told me that he and Robert met first and then they were introduced to senator Gatewood," said Sandra.

"Sandra it seems you are holding something back, if you are, please tell me," said Nicole.

"Nicole, you are a very perceptive person. The Vietnam War deeply affected Mark in so many ways. He ended up on a psychiatrist couch trying to find a solution to the bad dreams he was having after the war. He would wake-up in a cold sweat in the middle of the night after seeing images of the war dancing in his head and seeing so many people getting killed. Mark isn't a deranged lunatic by any stretch of the imagination. We heard all the stories about Agent Orange and how it affected the people who fought in the war. I strongly felt the war robbed Mark of the most precious years of his life," said Sandra.

"I know exactly what you mean," said Nicole.

"Mark has never told anyone this beside me and it took him a long time to even tell me. But you have a right to know because Robert was your husband," said Sandra.

"Know what," said Nicole.

"How Mark feels responsible for Robert's death," said Sandra.

"Feels responsible for Robert's death in what way," said Nicole.

It was Mark's assignment to go on the air raid that night to bomb the enemy targets when Robert's B29 went down. He was feeling ill from an anxiety attack. Robert stepped right in his place and was the navigator. Several planes were shot down and several of the crew bailed out. Some of them were captured and held prisoner until the end of the war. The others apparently died and were presumed dead along with Robert. Some of things he encountered or saw were frightening. He said some of the serviceman had to actually cover themselves with other dead bodies as a camouflage to hide themselves from the enemy. He was ashamed to tell anyone and when Robert's B29 was confirmed shot down; Mark went into a state of depression. He was a mess, a complete mess when he came back from Vietnam. I didn't know what to do. I didn't want to leave him, but the thought did cross my mind. I love Mark with every fiber of my being, for good or worst and I decided to stand by him through all of this madness. Nicole I hope you are not mad, but I wanted to take this time to tell you what Mark actually went through after the war and he is still fighting those demons. Mark would no more ever be the same," said Sandra.

"Sandra, I am not mad, if anything I'm numb."

"Mark went into a state of depression after the war. He had Robert's death all bottled up inside. As I said earlier, he would wake-up in the middle of the night screaming Robert's name. Yelling, "it should have been me, it should have been me, and I'm sorry Robert." I didn't know what in the world he was talking about, but I knew the name Robert meant something to him. As I said earlier, he spent countless hours on a psychiatrist couch trying to find him self or better yet trying to come to grips with Robert's death. We had to be honest with ourselves to know that a few hours lying on someone's couch is not enough to wipe out bad experiences which will last a lifetime," said Sandra.

"Sandra, Mark shouldn't blame himself for Robert's death. That's a hell of a burden to carry around on anyone shoulders. He didn't make Robert get on that fighter plane. Robert made that choice. The one thing I admired about Robert is that he did everything he could to help his fellow man. Robert was ready and willing to defend his country's honor. He believed in patriotism. The war personally destroyed a lot of lives. It may have seemed senseless to you and I. They shared something in Vietnam we may never understand in this lifetime. Then again maybe it's not up to us to understand.

The Vietnam War was something that happened and we just have to live with it. For people like you and I, unfortunately we just have to deal with it for the rest of our lives. It is easy to sit back and point fingers; the war had a lingering effect on all Americans in one- way or another. As harsh as it may sound we just have to move on and deal with it. I wouldn't dare hold Mark personally responsible for Robert's death. Robert was his own man and died for his country."

"Nicole you are a class act. Even though it seems Mark has moved on. I don't think he will ever get over Robert's death. Robert meant too much to him. He has gotten better, but at times he has these flashbacks which could lead into a state of depression if he's not careful."

"That's good to hear that he's gotten better. Its good to know that you are here for him," said Nicole.

"Yeah, it been tough, but we have managed. Mark finally got his degree in political science from the University of Texas after he returned from the war. After the war he and senator Gatewood got involved in the political arena to help change the way Vietnam Veterans were treated after the war," said Sandra.

It was eight o'clock and the concert was about to start. The limo pulled up to the stadium and Nicole and Sandra were escorted to the stadium elevator to the luxury skyboxes. Nicole later found out that they were special guest of Mr. Willie Nelson, Mr. Nelson song some of his greatest hits, plus some songs from his new album.

After the concert Nicole felt that Mr. Nelson put on a hell of a show, a heart stopper, but more importantly the concert was for a good cause. Nicole and Sandra went backstage to actually meet the entertainer. Mr. Nelson thanked them for coming out for this worthy cause. Farmers in America were ailing because of poor crop production and were about to become an endangered species. Nicole took a few snap shots with the entertainer.

Sandra presented the entertainer with a proclamation on behalf of his humanitarian efforts from the Texas state legislation. Senator Thread had introduced a bill in the senate for farmers who had loss their land due to bankruptcy or whatever reason to buy back their land at a reasonable price with extremely low interest rates. Farmers had been in dismay for some years due to Mother Nature that produced bad crop production as they were stripped of their land and allowed to pay a high interest rate for land they use to own. Farmers were crying foul filing lawsuits after lawsuits against the government because they felt the government cared more about space cadets, sending man to the moon while the real warfare was down on earth.

Mr. Nelson explained to Sandra and Nicole how he was on a mission, dedicated to helping the farmers. He autographed pictures and gave them to Sandra and Nicole. He also took the time to do some networking as he talked to Nicole about getting corporate America more involved in his efforts. Nicole promised him her sincere efforts in doing so. Nicole informed Mr. Nelson that Maywell is concerned about the farmer's welfare as well as environmental issues, but vowed Maywell would do more to help the cause.

The limo left the stadium and took Sandra and Nicole to the banks of the Colorado River for a firework display. This was a common event on the fourth of July. The event blended in well with Austin's illuminated moonlight tower lights. A twenty-seven 150-feet iron frame topped with mercury vapor lamps that painted the skyline blue.

Nicole enjoyed every moment because it seemed magical and the fourth of July was her favorite holiday when she was a kid. She enjoyed playing with fireworks as a kid and eating good southern barbecue and homemade ice cream when she visited her aunt's house down south. Nicole was filming the event with her camcorder. Her camcorder was her bible and she took it on every trip because she had a video library at home. Nicole and Robert always wanted a video library in their home so if and when they had kids they could show them all the exciting places they had been.

Nicole and Sandra quietly got back in the limo and directed the driver to Threadgills, a famous Austin bar and grill for a nightcap. Sandra informed Nicole that the President would be arriving in the morning on Air Force One and extended Nicole an invitation to attend a dinner at the governor's mansion, an invitation Nicole kindly accepted.

It was Thursday and the forecast called for a beautiful day. The senator's guest promptly arrived on schedule. The guest list included the President, Nicole, Texas's governor, Mary Dupree, and some of senator Thread's party constituents like senator Gatewood.

Nicole arrived early as the governor took her and Sandra on a tour of the governor's mansion. The mansion housed some important history of Texas. There was a portrait on the wall of Stephen Fuller Austin. The portrait was a perfect rendition of Mr. Austin, while the governor took Nicole and Sandra on tour the rest of the guest stood around mingling.

Everyone at the dinner ate a health conscience meal. The President had made health one of his primary issues during his campaign in trying to get fellow Americans to eat and exercise properly. The President made it a routine to jog three miles every morning whenever he got the chance. These types of issues were discussed over dinner.

After dinner the guest all adjourned from the dining room and went into a conference room. There they engaged in small talk from everything from sports to politics. The men were talking about sports and the women you name it they talked about it. The President and the governor made a friendly wager on who will win the division this fall between the Dallas Cowboys and the Washington Redskins. The governor was a Cowboy fan and indicated that Dallas would win their third straight super bowl this decade. The President was a Redskins fan and said the road to the super bowl would have to come through D.C. They made a friendly wager, the loser would have to buy the winner a turkey and give them a half dollar. It was an unusual bet, but they both accepted it. The governor was bragging about how everything is big in Texas. He had good reason to gloat because the Houston Rockets had just won their first NBA championship and he indicated they would repeat following year. It had been a big year in professional sports in Texas and the governor loved it. He went as far as stating he had something to do with it.

The fund-raiser the next day was just as impressive if not better. Senator Thread raised over a million dollars for his re-election campaign with a small portion going to charity. The President was a natural for the public eye and gave one of his chilling speeches that had people on their feet and their hands in their pockets.

As Nicole was sitting there hanging on the President's every word, she was informed that she had an emergency phone call in the lobby. The phone call totally caught her off guard. The phone call was from the bearer of bad news himself so it seemed none other than Mr. John Aslong.

"Nicole you need to get back to the office at once," he said in a stern voice.

"Oh John what is it now," said Nicole.

"I rather not get into over the phone. I rather wait until you get here," he said.

Nicole knew it was serious more so than the last time he beckons her to come back to the office. All she could think about was the Warsaw contract with the Pentagon and said to her self, "no not again." A still voice said to her," stay calm and don't read to much into it," she was having a good time and really didn't need to know all the details right anyway. This will have to wait until she arrives back at the office. She remembered so vividly Robert saying to her "brush all problems off your shoulders."

"Okay John I will be on the first flight in the morning."

By the time the fund-raiser was over and the guest had started to leave her attention immediately turn back to the office. "No not again" she shouted to herself. Sandra approached her and ask her was everything okay. They were to go shopping tomorrow. Nicole informed her she would have to take a rain check because she had to leave and head back to the office.

The flight back home was a somber one, more so than the last time she was summoned back to headquarters concerning the Moltra and Kincade debacle and this was getting old. It seemed as though a calamity would strike every time she would go out of town. Was she getting paranoid? All she could say is "No not again" because it wasn't a damn thing she could do about it. These recent setbacks weren't in the job description when she took this damn job, neither was the word fool either, because a person would have to be crazy to take on this kind of responsibility, but in a subtle way they are part of the job description. It is in the fine print that people often look over. Nicole wasn't a big enough fool not to realize that the stakes were high and these types of setbacks come with the territory as she previously realized with the Moltra and Kincade deals. She wanted to think happy thoughts. As she looked out the window of the plane she saw this picturesque view of the clouds with no descriptive shape or form and immediately she felt a sense of calmness.

Back at the house she was tired but couldn't sleep. She decided to read some motivational books she had stored away in the attic about positive thinking. She felt she needed this before she would have to confront the firing squad tomorrow. As she was sifting through some books she came across some love letters from Robert during their courtship and even while they were married. In one letter in particular Robert wrote, when they were married and he was away on a business trip he asked Nicole for a date when he returned back home. "I miss you," Robert stated with emphasis "and once I return home I will grab you and kiss you from head to toe, every inch of your body so I can taste the sweetness of your perfume which is definitely not sweeter than you. I can see you now; you look wonderful as I gaze into your beautiful eyes. Life is no fun when you are not around and as I sit here, all I can think about is the things I would like to do to you."

Nicole had a smile on her face bigger than the state of Texas. The night Robert returned home, Nicole remembered that night like it was yesterday, that was a great night to say the least. They wined and dined at an expensive restaurant, went dancing and stayed out until the wee hours of the morning. Once they returned home the rest was history for they made love like they never had made love before.

Nicole had a special connection to those letters; the letters were all the motivation she needed. She got so caught up reading the letter she forgot about the motivational book she intended to read. Those letters made her happy and made all her problems, though it seemed, go away. But nothing could take the place of the memories she shared in her heart for that man. This particular night she took the letter to bed with her and quietly fell asleep.

CHAPTER
15

On a Thursday afternoon, Maywell board members called a meeting at shareholders and investors request to find out what went wrong in losing the Warsaw contract to Conquest. It was a meeting of the minds to counteract and develop a strategy to this latest setback. The meeting was a somber one as Nicole was prepared to turn in her resignation. Though she'd never been a quitter a person could only take so much and this is simply not worth it. She didn't care what people would think, that a woman simply could not handle the day- to-day responsibilities of running a major corporation. She knew her critics would say, "I told you so. This is a man's world, the big game, and a woman is simply not cut out for this." She had too much on her plate already to think about, trying to come to grips with the circumstances surrounding Robert's death. Her motto was to expect the unexpected as her head could have easily been on the chopping block. She knew all fingers would be pointed at her and just maybe she had lost the support of the board this time. She knew if old man Maywell was living she knew that her ass would be good as gone. She felt it is not worth this and she gave it her best shot, at least she tried. She could not believe she was feeling this way, like a sore loser. This is how quitters thinks, and damn it she is no quitter. She had a lot of questions ringing in her head, but no answers. The only thing she knew is quitting wasn't an option. If they wanted her out they would have to kick her ass out.

At the meeting, board members were looking at the morning headlines in the Wall Street Journal and Forbes magazine that read, "Conquest Does It Again". The article went on to read that Conquest is a force to be reckon with in the computer industry and at this rate will overtake Maywell in the next few years if Maywell doesn't get their act together and go back to the basics by doing the things it took in the beginning in becoming the world's number one computer company. The article went on to read that Maywell had lost its touch and is not as intimidating as it once was. Maywell has become too soft. Nicole felt that critics were taking pot shots at her, nothing less than character assassination, by using the word soft and she being a woman. Hell it seemed like they were writing her obituary. Damn, "life can be so cruel," she thought. The article gave a lot of suggestions on what went wrong and what Maywell should do to keep its place as being the number one computer company in the world. This was the type of crap that would make old man Maywell turn over in his grave. No one dictated to him on how to run his business, he was the dictator. He didn't read this type of bullshit because he did things his way and his way only and if you didn't like it you could simply go to hell. Old man Maywell often stated he would meet you there if necessary. He could get down and dirty with the best of them and lower than a snake belly crawling in a rout.

The aftermath of losing the defense contract did create a hostile environment within the ranks of the company that sent shock waves throughout the industry and on Wall Street. Maywell still hadn't recovered over losing the Moltra and Kincade contracts. This was a first for Maywell, a company that always gotten what they wanted. Other companies always use to literally beg to do business with them. One thing Ty Dannerman had in his favor is that Maywell never lost a deal under his tenure. Although there was internal strife, which all companies do have at one time or another because of egos, which rears its ugly head from time to time, but nothing like this. Ty's image led him to his doom. He also had some financial factors in his favor. Maywell had always stood on solid ground, a cash cow, a great bastion when it came to money matters. Now it seems that this great bastion has fallen flatter than a penny, but not with some help from none other than Mr. Dannerman himself.

Mr. Dannerman and Mr. McRand had hired Courtney Asmail, a woman of the night who specializes in intriguing favors to entertain Mr. Bill Cordova, the top Pentagon official. Ms. Asmail was on Mr. McRand's payroll. She was Artie's trump card, his ace in the hole whenever he needed the knockout punch. Ms. Asmail was his heavy hitter. She specialized in having tryst with the movers and shakers in corporate

America. Courtney was a close ally of old Artie for years. Art, being the so-called religious person that he is, he knew that women had been offering sexual favors since time began in order to bring a man to his knees and have him squealing like a pig caught under a fence, begging for mercy until he looks silly. This was a mere case of blackmail.

Ms. Asmail threatened to sue Mr. McRand years back on sexual harassment charges if he didn't pay her a cash settlement and keep her on his payroll. Mr. McRand paid Ms. Asmail $450,000 in cash, hush money and promised her a job for life with Conquest only if she would be loyal to him in his corporate endeavors. She didn't go public with the sexual harassment suit and made a pack with the devil. This didn't make sense because the two had a stormy relationship for years; she was his administrative assistant, which meant she administered to his every need. She was somewhat qualified for the position because she had worked at Conquest since she was an intern in college and graduated with honors.

Courtney was the men's pet and the women's regret because she was a very attractive woman with skills. She perfected those skills by lying mostly on her back. McRand informed her to go to D.C. to entertain Mr. Cordova and utilize her skills to the fullest. McRand had done his homework because he knew Cordova was a serious womanizer. Cordova would go out on a limb for sex. He used the power of his office for his own personal gain. McRand knew it took a sleaze to know a sleaze. Mr. Cordova was truly a sleaze ball.

Ms. Asmail met Mr. Cordova at a bar outside D.C. in Virginia, a circumstance meeting. Mr. Cordova was at the bar waiting for the bartender to bring him a drink. Cordova had an arrogance about himself as Courtney arrived. He could have done one or two things, buy her a drink and said goodnight or tap dance with her. He chose the later because it sounded more enticing. He knew his wife was waiting at home, but didn't give a damn because he had the perfect alibi, he worked long hours and he couldn't discuss his work with anyone in fear of violating U.S. security laws.

Ms. Asmail casually walked up to the bar and approached Mr. Cordova and he bought her a drink.

"Are you Courtney?" Mr. Cordova asked, like he didn't already know. She had told him what she would be wearing.

"Yes, I am and you are Mr. Cordova," as they kept it very formal.

They moved over to a table in the corner of the bar behind some plants. Soft jazz music was playing in the background.

"What your angle Ms. Asmail?" said Mr. Cordova as he didn't know. He wasn't the one to mince words. He didn't like to beat around the bush.

"Why Mr. Cordova, my angle is the same as any beautiful woman, satisfaction. We can leave this place and I can give you a clearer picture and you yourself can literally see all my angles," said Ms. Asmail.

She crossed her legs and smiled at him with her seductive eyes. The temperature was literally rising. She kicked her shoes off and rubbed her feet gently across his thigh. When she touched him he basically lost control. He was a puppet on a string. She knew she had him right where she wanted him. He was slightly intoxicated, not from the alcohol, but from her spell. She was dangerous like a poisonous spider and he was trapped in her web, a web of deceit that is. He glanced at the clock as though he had to be somewhere. He went to the pay phone and made a call and returned to the table. He took Courtney by the hand as they headed out the door. They went back to her hotel room. They engaged in some stimulating conversation, something about world affairs.

"Would you like a drink?" asked Courtney.

"Yes," he replied.

She had fixed him a hurricane as she had a margarita. Courtney slipped on something more comfortable while putting on some soft romantic music. She moved closer with her right hand rubbing gently across his face while stroking all his pressure points while her breast was pressed against his chest. The time had come to cut through all the foreplay. Mr. Cordova was a male chauvinist pig and he knew Ms. Asmail was working for Conquest on behalf of trying to get the Warsaw contracts from Maywell, which in his mind was a done deal. He wanted to do business with Maywell because he wanted to get next to Nicole. He nearly lost it when he met with Nicole. Her stunning beauty along with the scent of her perfume literally drove him wild. The only thing he could think about was what he wanted to do to Nicole. But right now he wanted to take care of the business at hand. He engaged in sex just like he wanted it, anytime, anytime the opportunity presented itself.

After their rump in the sack, Bill lit a cigarette. Courtney smiled and put on her silk robe and went to the closet. She reached up on the shelf as though she was looking for something. Bill heard a clicking sound and asked, what was that noise? Courtney just played coy and said she dropped her earring. She had this innocent look on her face and Bill rolled back over and continued smoking his cigarette. Courtney made her way back to the bed to engage in some small talk.

"How long have you been at the Pentagon Bill?" asked Courtney.

Mr. Cordova was very vague and not to mention ready to go because his wife was waiting at home for him.

"A lifetime he shouted. Look we both got what we wanted now its time to say goodbye. It was my pleasure, you are good, damn good as a matter of fact, your skills are superb, and to bad you have to waste your life away in corporate America. You could make a name for yourself doing what you do best. See yah, until the next time we meet again."

He threw some money on the table thinking all women love to have money after sex as he walked out the door. Ms. Asmail fell back on the bed with a grin and said to her self, "no Mr. Cordova the pleasure has been all mind."

The next day a Federal Express package arrived at Mr. Cordova office at precisely ten o'clock a.m. eastern standard time. His secretary signed for the package and took it in to him. He was in the process of finalizing the Warsaw contract with Maywell as visions of Nicole danced in his head. He took the package and had that what in the hell is this expression on his face. He knew it was safe because the package had to clear security for the fear of biological chemicals. The Pentagon was prepared for biological warfare. He opened the package and low and behold it was a videotape. He wasn't expecting anything, so this caught him totally off guard. He closed his door and popped the video in the VCR.

As he watched the tape, a dull nervous feeling throbbed in the pit of his stomach. On the tape was his lovemaking tryst with Ms. Asmail. He almost fainted. The tape had the date and time of the actual tryst. At the end of the tape Ms. Asmail recorded a small message and repeated his famous words, "the pleasure was all mine and I think you know what this means, if not hopefully you will figure it out. Conquest looks forward in being rewarded the Warsaw contract. And have a nice day."

Mr. Cordova repeated those famous last words, "The bitch set me up."

He couldn't dispose of it because he knew there were other copies. This could destroy him personally and professionally if the tape fell into the wrong people hands.

He wanted to retire in a couple of years, but if he lost his job, there goes his pension, plus he would be stripped of his rank. He was a high-ranking official at the Pentagon. Bill realized he had been had and had bad. After all the women he had slept with, time had finally caught up with him. He had no other choice but to reward the Warsaw contract to Conquest.

CHAPTER 16

Sitting at home contemplating her future Nicole refused to feel sorry for her self after losing the Warsaw contract to Conquest. Even though she still had the support of the board this was a hard pill for her to swallow. She needed a distraction. She turned on the TV, flipping through the channels, there was nothing on that caught her immediate attention, but the news and it was depressing. "Damn," she thought to herself I can't win for losing. It had been a long day and she realized she hadn't eaten anything the entire day even though she didn't have an appetite. She was just too discouraged to eat.

The evening was still young. Nicole took a shower, got dressed and went to the club for dinner. Even though she didn't feel like being sociable she knew she needed to eat. Plus, it was jazz night at the club and it would do her good to get out. As she was getting dressed the phone ranged.

"Hello Nicole this is Ty," the voice said on the other end.

Now, this was a surprise, literally left Nicole breathless because Ty hardly ever said two words to her at work let alone call her.

"Yes Ty, this is a pleasant surprise how may I help you," said Nicole.

"I was just calling to let you know that you still have the board's full support and that no one blames you for what has happen recently by us losing those deals to Conquest. I wanted to tell you that after the meeting today, but didn't have the opportunity. These types of things happen in business from time to time even though Maywell has never experienced them, we just have to accept them because times are changing and there are too many unforeseen forces, the economy has been very unfriendly, and the environment, etc. You name it and we have to contend with it. We are operating in a new era and even old man Maywell would have trouble dealing with things today, even though he wouldn't admit it. Keep your head up. Remember its business and nothing personal."

"Thanks Ty I appreciate your support, it really means a lot to me," said Nicole.

Nicole was in pure shock she didn't know what to expect from that call. She wondered what in the hell was that all about. At the club Nicole ordered her usual. The band started to play a rendition of Stanley Jordan's old tunes. The music and the food were good, very good as a matter of fact. The place was crowded, but it was to be expected because it was jazz night. Nicole really was enjoying herself even though Ty's phone was very puzzling to her; she refused to let it ruin her night. She exchanged pleasantries with some acquaintances at intermission.

Quickly her mind reverted back to Ty's phone call. The big sixty-four thousand question is why would Ty call her at home of all places? This was strange, very strange. "No dam it, Nicole don't make too much of out of this," she said to herself. She just didn't know what to make of the call. She had heard a lot of things about Ty like he only does things if something is in it for him, but she wanted to give him the benefit of the doubt. Just maybe it was just a friendly gesture to say the least, nothing more nothing less. After all he did sound sincere, but most people do when they want something. She remembered what her mother use to always say, "Always follow your first mind, trust your instincts and if something stays on your mind more then ten minutes you got a problem." Her instincts told her something wasn't right. She needed a friend right now or someone she could trust. That person had always been her mother. But its time like these you have to stand on your own two feet. She didn't know who to trust or who to turn to. All she knew was this was a very complicated situation. She couldn't believe this. She was sitting here trying to enjoy herself, but was totally distracted, the things that was running through her mind. "This is not real," she said to herself. It seems like the only logical thing to do was to talk to her self. Could she come up with a better idea?

"Yeah, just continue to do the things that are for the good of the company and through hard work everything will be all right, right? But what if they don't? She knew Maywell wouldn't tolerate the company continuing to lose deals under her tenure. Old man Maywell would literally resurrect from the grave and kick her ass to the curve himself if this continued, think about it Nicole. What if you fall flat on your face? You will be the laughing stock of the industry. What then? Should I just fade away with the sunset? especially when you have given your best shot. But wait Nicole doing the best you can do isn't necessarily doing your job is it? "This is crazy, Nicole. I guess I'm supposed to let things be, of course not. You are a fighter. At this moment I don't feel like much of a fighter. Sorry. Look, Nicole you have to be realistic about the situation. You have the board's approval so they say; they have tried to convince you of that. You can't stop the inevitable. If you are going to get ambushed, so be it. Just settle down and don't feel sorry for yourself. I guess talking to yourself is meaningful dialogue if you don't answer. It was like she had a good angel on her right shoulder and a bad angel on the left one warring against one another and she caught in the middle. The kind of shit you see on cartoons.

The band returned from intermission playing some Miles Davis's old tunes. A waiter asked Nicole if she needed anything and she politely answered no. She listened tentatively as the band played two more sets. It was getting late and she was tired. It was a fun filled time being at the club because it provided the atmosphere she needed, just to relax although she was somewhat distracted. She took the scenic route on the drive home. Once at home she had a nightcap, showered looked out of the window and thought to herself, "tomorrow is a brand new day then its back to the real world."

CHAPTER 17

all Street was buzzing. Maywell's numbers were still good after losing the Warsaw contract to their arc rival. Maywell stock took a little hit, but overall the numbers were pleasant to say the least. Board members were somewhat pleased at the numbers even though they didn't get the numbers they had projected. Industry analysts were totally surprised.

The past week had been brutal not to mention unproductive. Nicole needed time to reflect, a time to get away or be in exile it seemed. She felt the presence of old man Maywell breathing down her neck. She wanted to get away from the office. Away from the copiers, computers, and fax machines, etc. She was almost scared to leave the office because every time she leaves it seems like something bad happens. Most of all she wanted to get away from the people at the office sitting behind their desk drinking coffee or whatever. The office has become a rat race it seems since Maywell lost the Warsaw contract. People standing in groups by the water fountains and in the break room engaging in small talk wondering what went wrong, wondering will there be another shake-up at the company. No one it seemed could get any work done. People were waiting for the ball to drop. The murmurings were endless. The atmosphere at the office was morbid to say the least.

At home Nicole was looking at Maywell's closing numbers on Wall Street, which she thought was respectable, but still not good enough according to her standards. She felt that there was a lot of work that she needed to do. She knew she was pushing herself to the limit, but that was to be expected. She wanted to go thru some reports, but quickly decided against it because she was tired, mentally drained that is. For once she wanted to do something she wanted to do for a change. She thought about taking in a movie. Then a thought crossed her mind about going for a swim or doing some work around the house. She totally dismissed all those ideas because this particular day she just felt plain lazy. She liked the idea of going to the movies, but no movie has ever moved her like The Silence of the Lambs, her all time favorite movie. She had watched a lot of movies in her time, some good ones as a matter of fact, but nothing nearly as well as The Silence of the Lambs. She felt she had plenty of time to go for a swim or do some work around the house.

It was Friday and it had been a long week and the only thing she felt like doing was nothing, nothing at all. As she was channel surfing on the tube, Dr. Phil was talking about relationships on The Ophrah Winstone Show as usual. This was something that she could identify with since her and Robert had the ultimate relationship. Plus Dr. Phil kept it real as the say in the hip-hop world. Nicole strongly thought Dr. Phil was good enough to have his own talk show. She just felt Ophrah had some of the most interesting topics of any talk show host; her show was inspiring to all, unlike some of the other trashy talk shows looking to get high ratings.

When The Ophrah Winstone Show went off she came across this documentary that was airing on the history channel about Vietnam veterans that had fathered kids out of wedlock by Vietnamese women during the war who eventually returned to the States to be with their real families. How disgusting Nicole thought how these American men used these women to fulfill their own desires. This was mind bogging, not to pass judgment, but these American men were engaged in a physical war not a sexual one and they should have had one primary purpose in mind. This was not a pleasure trip. Nicole felt these men should have had enough decency to keep their private parts to themselves until they made it back home and not have to live a double life. Nicole felt there was no excuse as some of these men tried to justify their actions because they felt it was a good chance they may not make it back home. Then you should die with honor Nicole felt. Robert would have never cheated on her because he was an honorable man. She couldn't even picture this sort of thing ever happening to her. She knew she was the only woman in Robert's life. She trusted Robert with her life. She made a connection with the women who lost their spouses in the war, but couldn't imagine what the women who spouses fathered children were going through. This was unimaginable let alone forgivable.

Nicole felt the most compelling part of this documentary was how these kids were spitefully treated and made to serve with rigor because they were different. Members of their own families ostracize these kids. Some of these kids nearly lost their lives trying to escape this cruel treatment. The story went on to say that there were thousands of these kids abandoned by these American men. Some were even abandoned by their mothers and sold to people on the black market who were trying to become American citizens.

Nicole literally had tears in her eyes. Her heart went out to those kids. No one should have ever had to experience such treatment, let alone an innocent child who is not responsible for being here. Hell none of us are for that matter. During biblical times people have been tortured, sexually abused, and malnourished because they like look different on the outside. Mixed blood or not, all blood is still red. Discrimination expands across the globe and is not confined to one particular part of the world. Nicole couldn't help to wonder do dogs if they are half-breed or different than other dogs ostracize. No, they still play and breed together. Why can't people do the same Nicole felt? It seems animals have more sense then people. The sad part about it is that these people are generally affected for the rest of their lives. The memories are too painful until this very day. They interviewed some of these kids and they had to recollect painful details they experienced as a child. Nicole wondered how anyone could deal with those painful demons. One would have to have a strong spirit abiding in them and know what that spirit truly is in order to survive this kind of treatment.

The last part of the documentary focused on the effect of Agent Orange, chemicals American warplanes sprayed on the Vietnamese jungle to keep them from hiding. This chemical affected many people during the war. It is said to cause serious health problems and birth defects. The report went on to say that the people who was infected by this chemical is nothing more than a walking tomb to this very day.

After watching such a compelling piece, it made Nicole's problems seem minimal, putting her problems in perspective. Losing deals, which come and go, is one thing, but to actually live a life of torture is a whole different ballgame. You can always get another job, but messing with one's sanity is an injustice she felt.

CHAPTER
18

It was typical winter weather for New York. The snow covered the city, but the streets were clear. Nicole was glad to be home. She grew-up in nearby Purchase, New York. Everything seemed in tack. It had been a while since she last visited. She had promised her mother that she would visit soon when her mother came to visit her. What better time to visit New York than in the heart of winter?

A limo picked her up at the JFK airport and took her to her mother's house. Traffic was congested as usual and darkness was fast approaching. When she arrived at her mother's house her mother had left her a note on the refrigerator like she always used to do when she left the house when Nicole was growing up that she was over a friend house playing bridge. Nicole thought to her self "how something's never change," and when her mother is playing bridge with her monthly bridge club it could definitely take some time. These ladies make brownies and fix tea and talked about everything under the sun.

Nicole was glad her mother was involved in extra curricular activities since her father's death. These women were her mother's support group and her mother enjoyed being around them. After she unpacked, she put on her coat and drove her father's car to the mall. Her mother kept her father's car in remembrance of him and drove it occasionally. Her mother took good care of the vehicle.

What better place to go shopping than New York, the home of fashion! Even though Nicole like living in South Carolina, it's no place like home. It was something she just missed about home, like shopping for one. Shopping made her feel like she was worth something, then again it does that to most women. In the two hours she was gone she must to have bought out New York it seemed. She bought everything from lingerie to shoes. Nicole felt a woman could never have enough pairs of shoes because style changes and shoes defined a woman. Her closet was full of shoes.

It was getting late and she figured her mother probably had made it home. It felt so good to be home. It seemed like the only time she comes to the Big Apple is for business only. She was always in a hurry. Never had time to do the things she wanted to do, like shop. Visit the boutique shops; get her hair done, things of that nature.

When she turned in the driveway of her mother's home she saw the kitchen light on and Nicole immediately knew her mother had made it home. Before she could get in the door good her mother grabbed her and hugged her almost to death. It was one of those bear hugs.

"Expecting someone mother?" Nicole jokingly asked.

"Yeah, you silly," her mother said.

"How have you been doing mother?" asked Nicole.

"Great since you are here. I see I don't have to ask you that question seeing all those packages in your hands. You must have bought out the store or at least you tried to."

"Very funny mother I see you still have a sense of humor. You know what shopping does for me."

"Sure it makes you broke."

"Ha! Ha! mother very funny."

They both had a big laugh because they were very happy to see one another. Nicole put away her packages, slipped on something comfortable. Her mother had fixed dinner, all of Nicole's favorites by the way. After dinner her mother made some hot tea and they gathered around the fireplace. It was very cold outside and the snow was coming down heavy. Local forecasters had predicted three inches by the morning. This was their time, talking about old times. No discussions about Maywell or business was allowed whatsoever, it was off limits, just girlie talk. They talked to the wee hours of the morning and Nicole fell asleep in her mother's arms and her mother woke her up and told her to go to bed. Her mother was concerned, not worried about her daughter, like all mothers should feel about their kids, but knew if anyone could overcome adversity Nicole could. She taught Nicole that, meet your problems head on.

The next morning Nicole did some light early morning exercises. It was too cold to go jogging. She drank some carrot juice while eating an assortment of fruits along with some brand cereal.

"Mother do you have any big plans for today. If so don't let me stand in your way. I can find something to do. It just feels so good to be at home."

"I thought maybe we could do something together. Make sure you don't plan anything for tonight."

"Mother, what do you have up your sleeve? I know you got something going on."

"Well, I have something special planned for the both of us tonight."

"That's, fine, I was just going to call Andrea and see if we could get together later. I know she would be surprised to know I'm in town, if you haven't already told her. Plus, I want to see those twins. She would kill me if she knew I was in town and didn't stop by."

"You can go by her house to see the kids this afternoon. Just don't make plans for tonight. I have a surprise."

"Mother I can put off seeing Andrea until tomorrow. You know how I like surprises."

They went to the parlor and got a manicure, pedicure, and a massage. They had mud- packs put on their faces, relaxed in the sauna. They visited some boutiques had lunch. Nicole's mother had informed her that where they would be going tonight you had to dress formal. Her mother had purchase tickets to see the hit Broadway play, Fiddler on the Roof which was the hottest ticket in town. The show had been sold out for five consecutive months and tickets were hard to come by. Her mother had to pull some strings to get her hand on these tickets.

The show was a blast. Next Nicole's mother had also purchased some tickets to see none other then Whitney Houston playing at Madison Square Garden. Nicole was enjoying this.

"Mother you are the best mother a person could have."

"I know, but let's enjoy the concert. You have plenty of time to tell me that. Plus, I like hearing it."

It had been a long time since Nicole went to a concert. She loved Whitney Houston because she felt she was one of purest singer/entertainers out there. Whitney had crossover appeal loved by everyone, no matter what color you are. She has all of Whitney's CD's. She felt Whitney had paid her dues. The fact of the matter is Whitney's mom and her mom went to grade school together at one of the nation's upscale institutions during that time that had students from many different races. Even though they were different and came from different backgrounds they became close friends.

Whitney sang some of Nicole's all time favorites. Plus, Whitney sang some of Sarah's Vaughn's old tunes. The only thing Nicole could say after the concert is "The girl can sing." Despite her recent troubles and how the press had been ragging on her lately. Nicole could definitely identify with this. Just leave the woman alone if your main purpose is to just bring her down Nicole felt.

The next day she visited Andrea and gave the kids their gifts. Nicole and Andrea ran the streets like old times while Andrea's better half stayed at home with the kids. It was like a reunion. But any time those two got together it was pure fun. They shopped till they dropped. It was fun being home and for a moment she thought about turning in her resignation and returning home for good and go into business for herself. This is what life is supposed to be like, having fun and enjoying it. But she quickly realized people where counting on her.

But all good things must come to an end. She would have to savor the moment. The good thing about it she can always come back home because that's where the heart is.

CHAPTER
19

At seven a.m., Nicole was at her office going over reports for the third quarter. Maywell was still ahead of their competitors, thanks to operation Europe. By eight o'clock most of the employees had arrived at work. It was business as usual, people running down the halls with reports in one hand and coffee in the other. Phones and fax machines were ringing off the hook. It was like grand central station. Nicole loved every minute. "What a difference a day makes," she thought to herself. Just recently she wanted to resign, lick her wounds and ride off into the sunset. But something inside her wouldn't let that happen. She came to the conclusion that she would just have to rise above her problems, look down on them and just deal with it. Nothing bad happened this time while she was away.

Another thing Maywell had going in its favor was that Maywell had reduced its prices on their PC's. This marketing campaign worked like a genius. Sales were up. Nicole had summoned James in marketing to her office to get some last minutes figures on the campaign.

"James what are the bottom line numbers on the PC campaign," said Nicole.

"Nicole, I'm way ahead of you, I put the report on your desk last night because I knew you would ask for them when you returned," said James.

"I'm sorry James here they are, right under my nose. If it had been a snake it would have bit me.

Nicole knew James was very trustworthy.

"Nicole as you can tell by the numbers the campaign is doing very well. Sales are up. It started off kind of shaky, but picked-up steam as time went on."

"Great, that's music to my ears. We need some good news around here for change in spite of our recent misfortunes," said Nicole.

"Yeah I know what you mean Nicole, things have been pretty wild around here lately, which is very unusual," said James.

"James, tell me something, you just took the words out of my mouth when you said things have been unusual around here lately. In your years here at the company, never mind I don't want to seem paranoid."

"What Nicole, say what's on your mind," said James?

"Maywell has never lost deals like we recently have before. Companies use to die to do business or just be associated with us. For the life of me I can't understand or may not ever understand why we lost those deals to Conquest of all people. Conquest was on shaky grounds with their questionable accounting practices that almost left them bankrupt. I know they have taken a turn for the better, but still, I just don't understand why anyone would want to be associated with them. Let alone do business with them," said Nicole.

There was a pause as James gazed up at the ceiling. Then he looked her straight in the eyes while biting his bottom lip.

"Nicole, it's like this, in my years here at Maywell, you are right nothing like this has ever taken place. I just don't have any answers. I wished I did. I just don't. I guess some things will always remain a mystery, but like I said earlier. It's very unusual how things have played out here recently. As the old saying goes, "it's a first time for everything." I know you can't worry about it. You have to keep on pressing on and maybe, just maybe things will be revealed later on down the line," said James.

"I know I must seem paranoid, but it more of a feeling that I have rather then a question and that bothers me. You know what I mean," said Nicole.

"Exactly, any one in your position would or should feel that way. Nicole I honestly believe Maywell's misfortunes had nothing to do with you. Things have been a little bizarre around here lately I must admit. It's just the nature of the business, nothing personal. Things happen that we have no control over. The economy, market trends, you name it. But I'm sure you have heard all this before," said James.

"Yeah, you are right. I have heard all of this before. But what sticks out in my mind is whom we lost them to Conquest of all people. Do you think it was a mere coincidence James?"

"Well, like a stated earlier, some things just don't have an explanation. It's like a crime going unsolved and the guilty party never gets charged for the crime. Some things in life remain a mystery, "said James.

"I know you are right, but I just feel, hell I don't know how I feel. I just know old man Maywell wouldn't be pleased," said Nicole.

"Nicole, I know I might sound repetitious, but you can't beat yourself up over this. Let bygones be bygones," said James.

"Somehow I feel I let the company down," said Nicole.

"Nicole all you can do is do the best you can do. That's it," said James.

"But sometimes the best you can do is not necessarily doing your job, is it?"

"Nicole people around here know what is expected of you. You are the one who is putting that added pressure on yourself. Just let it go," said James.

Nicole was thinking about the money she was making. Maywell didn't pay her a handsome salary and all those benefits that come along with it just to fail. If not the board, investors and shareholders would be screaming for her hide, threatening to boot her out the door. She felt life was funny that way. She always made it a point to cover her back. Ty was months behind in his work, took days off at his own will and Maywell never lost a deal. Just the opposite for her, her work was caught up and when she took time off something bad happens. Her timing was not great.

She opened her desk drawer looking for a file. She could use a drink right about now if she were a drinker. She knew she was cut out to do this. She had prepped for this all her life. As she looked down at the reports on her desk, they became a blur. She kept her composure, trying hard to concentrate. She took her reading glasses off, rubbed her temples with both hands as though she felt a migraine coming on. She hadn't had a migraine in along time, but had her migraine medication, Imitrex at hand because the pain can be intense at times at the onset. She didn't like to take medication unless she really had to. When these migraine starts she get nauseated, as though she needed to throw-up plus her eyes are very sensitive to light. She closed her eyes, but she wasn't dizzy. Without the Imitrex she can't function. She wouldn't wish this kind of pain on her worst enemy. The Imitrex stops the pain immediately. She ate some of lunch she had leftover from the night before. Nicole didn't want to take the Imitrex on an empty stomach because, that would make matters worst.

She wanted to go home but realized she needed to keep working. The office seemed as though it was closing in on her. As the evening went on she felt worst. She went to the bathroom washed her face in cold water. This made her feel somewhat better as she returned to the office. She turned to the first section of the file looking at the numbers as though she was studying to take an exam. The numbers were self explanatory, detailed to the letter. James really was a dependable guy and very valuable to the company. Under his guidance the marketing department was on top of their game. He was a one-man general in the department. James knew marketing, but also knew the legislation lingo that surrounded advertising. He was very strategic. He had laid everything out for Nicole. Nicole looked over the numbers like she expected them to change. She needed a break. More like a distraction. She walked over and looked out the window and saw a star. Not just any star, this star seemed to outshine all the others. As she gazed up at this star she made a wish. Something inside her said not to give-up on Robert. Immediately she felt his presence as she touched her wedding ring. She still wore the ring until this day, but that didn't stop men from hitting on her. Nicole's wedding ring was a magnet. It drew men to her. She felt those sorry ass men didn't give a damn as long as they got what they wanted. The only time she took off the ring was to clean it. As she thought of her and Robert's life together she got misty eyed. A cold chill ran down her spine. She begins to shiver. She stared at the star as though she expected it to fall, but it didn't. She heard a voice say within "patience Nicole, be patient for now."

CHAPTER 20

Nicole was on a conference call with Aaron about Maywell venturing into North and South Korea. Aaron had been researching and gathering information for the past year or so concerning this matter. Angela, one of Nicole's secretaries was right by Nicole's side taking the information in shorthand as Aaron seemed to be near on the voice animated system. Dinner was ordered, but no one found time to eat. It was around midnight before they called it a night. Before they left the office, Angela gave Nicole a brown brochure. The brochure contained Nicole's itinerary concerning Nicole's trip to Ho Chi Minh City's finest hotel. She had already booked Nicole's reservation the day before.

Nicole was to attend a high profile seven-day trade summit with some of the world's top leaders and business executive concerning business ventures into North and South Korea. This was because trade barriers and sanctions were recently lifted due to North and South Korea signing a nuke freeze agreement. At the summit there were protesters outside the meeting hall causing a scare demonstrating or denouncing the recent trade agreement signed by both parties. This was because of economic reasons, which the Koreans called it an unequal exchange. A local newspaper in Korea called the agreement a bunch of gibberish or hogwash. Some protestors were seriously hurt as one person died as they clashed with security. Security was beefed up to protect the people who attended the summit. Protestors were burning flags in the streets while chanting anti-Semitic remarks protesting the summit. The U.S. and the rest of the world had a chilly relationship with North and South Korea before they agreed to sign the agreement. Now it seems that North and South Korea were willing to become part of the free world as they planned to progress into the next millennium.

Nicole was busting with confidence after talking to Aaron. She told the board that Maywell could start expanding into North and South Korea by the end of the following year. North and South Korea wanted to improve their gross national product. Neither country didn't have a stock market, but was now attracting mutual-fund investors hoping to strike gold. Their population had increased dramatically since the Vietnam War when the communist government there began free market reforms. Their economy increased seven percent the past year due to the countries exported goods.

Aaron had informed Nicole that his research showed that investors would pour an estimated hundred and fifty billion into both countries by the new millennium. At that current pace, both countries will become a diamond in the rough, a gold mine according to recent money market studies. Maywell's shareholders were concerned about the current nuclear arms agreement between the U.S. and North and South Korea, which allows strict restrictions on foreign trade. The U.S. Commerce department had put pressure on the President to lift all trade sanctions with both countries. This was because both countries weren't cooperating fully with the U.S. when it came to MIA's during the Vietnam War. Nicole had talked briefly with the President when she was in Austin, Texas about the sanctions levied against North and South Korea.

The President informed Nicole that there was no exact timetable to when the sanction would be lifted because Congress was divided on the issue along party lines. Congress was the President's biggest foe because they basically shot down every piece of legislation he tried to introduce. He indicated to Nicole that the U.S. Commerce department had made great strides into improving business relations with both countries. The President credited U.S. Commerce secretary, Bobby Rowin for spearheading the trade agreement with both countries and that a major breakthrough should be forthcoming.

The Wall Street Journal quoted Nicole as saying, "North and South Korea are countries with tremendous growth potential and Maywell will lobby on Capitol

Hill to help Congress breakthrough legislation to open up trade agreements with both countries."

Maywell had made inroads through its research into both countries concerning trade agreements and market trends. They wanted to create a partnership rather than a business climate.

Nicole was reluctant to visit Ho Chi Minh City because of personal feeling concerning the war. They had changed somewhat due to modernization and economic development, which had a direct impact on Southeast Asia. Hopefully Maywell will have the same impact there as they had in Europe with Sparcomat. The government in North and South Korea would hopefully have an open mind when it comes to modern technology.

Maywell wanted to generate an intercontinental trade that would allow them to set-up a computerized network from England to North and South Korea. This would create jobs in both countries and hopefully eliminate sweatshops that employ under age kids. These sweat shops have put both countries in an economic recession.

·········

While sitting in her hotel room, Nicole was watching a Vietnamese news report that indicated that MIA's searches were picking up due to the sanctions lifted with both North and South Korea signed the nuke freeze agreement. "Here we go again," she thought to herself. The news report reported that Vietnam was making steady progress in gathering and processing information on MIA's who fought in the war.

The U.S. wanted documented proof that progress was being made. The U.S. wanted documents, photographs, dog tags, and other evidence deemed necessary to settle MIA's cases in a timely manner.

While looking at the published report the station showed a concentration camp, which some MIA's were held during the war. One man Nicole saw that flashed across the tube looked just like Robert. Nicole almost fainted, within an instant anxiety set in.

"No Nicole you didn't see that, it's your imagination playing tricks on you. You saw what you wanted to see. That couldn't have been Robert. No it wasn't. Dam it I know what I saw, right? Hell no! Stop it; just stop it. Oh my goodness here we go again. The same shit, but a different song, you are losing it Nicole, get a grip, you are going to end up on someone's couch if you keep it up. Its okay to talk to your self, just don't answer, right?" As the voice kept ringing in her head it got louder and louder so much so she felt a migraine coming on. She took some Imitrex to ease the pain.

The next morning after she cried herself to sleep, Nicole realized she needed some help. She realized a pattern was developing; she was talking to herself more frequently. But who could help her. All she knew was that as soon as she got back to the States she would contact senator Gatewood and inform him of what she saw. This was the kind of shit that would make a person lose their mind. She had heard and seen stories of people who lost love ones in the war who literally lost their minds and go into a state of depression because they fail to give up hope. She once met an elderly woman who said, "If she lived to get an hundred an four she would never give up hope that her son was still alive until this day." This woman was stricken with Alzheimer's. Nicole felt she was inches away from lying on a psychiatrist couch.

CHAPTER

21

Conquest stole Maywell's thunder and knocked the wind out of their sails once again when it launched its brand new PC onto the market first, way ahead of schedule. The PC got rave reviews and was selling like hotcakes at a reasonably low price. Maywell had planned to introduce their PC on the market first, but was stunned when Conquest beat them to the punch. The big question was how did Conquest get privileged information that Maywell was planning on launching a brand new PC on the market? Conquest was focusing their efforts totally on mainframe computers. Plus, they were still riding high on their recent fortunes with the Moltra and Kincade deals they stole from Maywell. They would have had to know at least a year or so in advance because Maywell hadn't put out published reports concerning their product line. Maywell liked to keep people in the dark. Everything about them is a mystery, to catch or throw people off guard. That was old man Maywell's claim to fame. Damn, the people at Maywell thought this was very strange. They didn't mean to be superstitious, but when it rains it pours, seemed like everything comes in threes whether it's good or bad. They wondered is that old saying true that every dog has his day.

Maywell's board members had a lot of questions, but no answers. Is this a mere coincidence? Some at the company felt it wasn't, but they couldn't prove it. Conquest PC had some of the same features as Maywell, a state of the art flat color monitor with a powerful microprocessor. The PC had more storage space with a larger battery capacity.

Ty loved every minute, seeing Maywell struggling to find answers. Revenge is so sweet he thought. What made it so gratifying was that all of this was his doing. It all started with a dinner date for two outside an English pub. A marriage made in heaven he called it. The participant was a Maywell engineer, who Ty had bribed that worked closely with Aaron on Sparomat. He informed the man that he would pay him enough to retire and that he would never have to work another day in his life. The other participant was on Art's payroll at Conquest. Ty had so much dirt on the engineer at Maywell that he pressured him to give Maywell's PC designs to Conquest. Plus, the man had very serious financial woes. The pressure was so great that the engineer ended up committing suicide.

The stakes were high, yet simple. All the engineer had to do was provide the computer designs to Artie's hitch man who would turn the information over to Conquest engineers. Artie had set-up a global spy network as a middleman to make it hard to trace any evidence back to him.

Ty was a very savvy businessman so he thought. He also covered his tracks. He wired money to foreign bank accounts, making it very hard to produce a money trail.

The spy network became unraveled due to a computer glitch. Aaron found it to be highly unusual that Maywell data systems, especially Sparomat were experiencing a lot of technical problems as of late. Aaron knew the programs like the backside of his hand. He had concluded research after research and became highly suspicious.

Aaron received an anonymous tip from a man, only known as Joe, which indicated that some powerful people were behind Maywell's recent misfortunes, which wanted to bring the company down. At a hefty price he would reveal that information. The man indicated that the less people involved the better. Aaron didn't want to get the police involved, not yet anyway because he didn't want to scare the man off. Plus, he wanted to resolve this as quickly as possible; he owed it to Nicole for having faith in him to head-up operation Europe. So he opted to take matters into his own hands.

Aaron had set-up a meeting with the man. He wanted to collect the information from the man and turn the evidence over to the police. Little did Joe know, he was being watched and after meeting with Aaron a bullet was enlarged in his skull? Ty knew the man had talked to Aaron and figured Aaron knew too much. Ty knew

Aaron would want to play the hero for Nicole's sake and ride in on his white horse and save the day. Nicole had him under her thumb. Ty didn't want to give Aaron the pleasure.

Ty wanted to get Aaron out of his hair once and for all. Ty had traced all of Aaron's phone calls while monitoring his every move, from Aaron's kitchen to his bathroom. Ty had Aaron under strict surveillance. Finally, a call was place to order the hit.

Aaron was getting off work late one night. He was headed to his car in the parking garage when two-masked gunman apprehended him. In an instant two bullet holes were pumped into his chest at close range, he died instantly.

The headline in the British tabloids the next morning read, 'Top Maywell Executive Found Murdered'. Aaron's wife knew something was wrong when Aaron didn't come home. He had called her from the office to notify her he was on his way home. His dinner was warming in the microwave. Nicole was distraught as she found out about Aaron's death from a phone call at home from the bearer of bad news himself, John Aslong.

Maywell's board members notified company employees of the unfortunate news as the flag was flown at half-staff at company headquarters. Nicole and the board members including Ty, who acted surprise, flew to London on the company jet to show support to Aaron's family. On the way to London Ty asked some of the board members who could something like this happen? He criticized the justice system for letting low life trash roams the streets preying on good citizens.

Once in London he notified Art and told him that the mission had been accomplished.

"Art it was a professional hit; no one would suspect a thing. The hit looked like it was an apparent robbery by two drug feigns looking for money," said Ty.

"Damn it Ty I didn't intend for things to go this far, someone at Maywell actually getting killed, even though Aaron had been a thorn in your side," said Art.

Art was highly upset at Ty. As an act of sympathy he resemblance a cross sign across his chest as he looks up toward the ceiling. He didn't want anyone killed as he thought about Aaron's family. Dying is a cowardly act he felt, the easy way out. His got his pleasure out of seeing people suffer. He wanted the people at Maywell to suffer just like he grandfather did. Seeing Maywell suffer is hitting them where it hurts the most, their wallet.

"Art don't wimp out on me now. Aaron had to be eliminated if we are going to continue on with our plans. He probably knew more than he should have," said Ty.

"I know, but," said Art.

"But nothing," said Ty. "Do you think old man Maywell felt sorry for literally killing your grandfather," said Ty.

"Ty we have had this conversation once before, I didn't won't this man's blood on my head. He had a family. Yes, I will be the first to admit I want to see them bastards at Maywell crawling on their knees, but I want them all to be breathing when that happens. If not, what's the point of all this. It won't be as gratifying if they are all dead, get the point," said Art. "Son of a bitch, damn it Art you want to be nice doing this ordeal. You can't have it both ways. I got to go. I got one hell of an acting job to do as I pay respect to Aaron's family with the other board members," said Ty.

"Yeah you get to almost act human," said Art.

Aaron body was flown back to the States. At the funeral his widow wore a black-laced dress while the kids tried to comfort their mother. It was especially hard on the youngest child. She was daddy little girl. The minister eulogized Aaron as a pillar of the community, a local boy that accomplished his dreams. Nicole wept, as she couldn't help to think about Robert and how Aaron's wife and kids must feel. Aaron was laid to rest in his hometown with a star banner salute.

Nicole immediately developed with the board's approval a scholarship fund in Aaron's name. Meanwhile Ty was getting richer by the minute. Art was paying him a commission off of Conquest latest fortunes along with a salary deposited into a Swiss bank account.

Nicole flew back to London to tie up loose ends on what Aaron had been working on. She would have to name a successor to replace Aaron, but she couldn't find the strengths to do it right now. Aaron was one of her biggest supporters when she first started with the company and the thought of replacing him seemed almost unconstitutional. No one would be as good as him in her mind. Aaron's wife flew to London with Nicole to clean out his office concerning his personal belongings. Nicole found a number of letters, faxes, and confidential documents in Aaron's office. She ran across a diary Aaron was keeping containing important documents. She figured it was research data Aaron had collected on Sparcomat.

The diary was written in codes; which Nicole knew nothing about. Some of the information he had written made sense. Aaron had written something about Maywell's recent misfortunes, which Nicole didn't readily understand. She put the diary in her briefcase and would read it in detail once she gets back to the States.

Aaron's diary indicated how much a certain informant was paid for information concerning Maywell's misfortunes. Information that other companies like Conquest had privilege to. Aaron went on to explain that some these informants pleaded guilty for accepting illegal payments for giving inside information, a trail of fraud and deceit Some of these informants were taken out of the way when they decided to turn over a knew leaf by cutting deals with the DA. Nicole was trying to make sense of all this. The question on her mind was why would Aaron keep something like this? What does this have to do with Sparcomat?

Could someone at Maywell be responsible? If so this would explain the company misfortunes. Who could she turn to or trust with this information inside the company? Immediately a voice within her said to tell no one for now.

Ty and Art knew that authorities were in hot pursuit of this spy network. London authorities were putting pressure on the DA to make an arrest in order to bring this network down. But every time they would get close someone would get taken out. London authorities were offering witness protection programs because bodies were being found execution style floating in river or cemented in concrete blocks all over Europe. Someone was dropping a dime on these people, which left London authorities puzzled.

Nicole took a flight back to London on the Concord because the information in Aaron's dairy was so intriguing. While in her hotel room at the Grosvenor House she received an anonymous letter. The letter read:

Dear Ms. Gershom:

"Please meet me for coffee at the local pub on 5th and Linden in an hour. Please come alone, I have some vital information that you will find beneficial concerning your colleague's death."

"P.S. I mean come alone and by yourself."

The letter wasn't signed. Nicole was very apprehensive. She didn't know what to make of the letter. Was this some kind of joke? If it is then it's not funny. Then she became very angry. Not fearing for her life. She wished the creeps could fry in hell for what they done. She knew Aaron's killers hadn't been bought to justice and she would do anything in her power to see these creeps put behind bars or better yet see them face the death penalty. So it was now her turn to play the hero and take matters into her own hands. She owed Aaron that much.

Nicole took a cab to the pub that was about fifteen minutes away from the hotel. The pub was on the outskirts of town. It was a rainy, cold dreary night, typical London weather.

Nicole had on her rain attire, something to serve as a camouflage. The letter didn't indicate what the informant would be wearing, so Nicole hoped he/she would recognize her. As she walked into the pub, it was dark with only a small crowd present. Most of the people in the pub were sitting at the bar, drinking beer and eating pretzels while watching a soccer game on the tub.

A waiter came up to Nicole and pointed to the informant sitting in the corner. The informant had on a wide black rim hat with dark sunglasses. Nicole hoped the man would get straight to the point. She didn't feel comfortable at all. The man said hello, but for the most part he was a man of few words.

"Madam you don't know me, but I know something about you," said the man.

Right their Nicole felt she was at a disadvantage, but she would let the man have his say.

Nervously the man got straight to the point, looking all around as though he was being followed. The man was paranoid as hell. This made Nicole nervous, very nervous as a matter of fact until she almost felt an anxiety attack come on, but she tried to maintain her composure. She was wondering what she had gotten herself into. She even started second guessing herself on whether she should have met the guy in the first place. She realized at this point that this was not a joke. It was serious, a life or death situation that she is now faced with.

"Art McRand became a wealthy business man which got his wealth the old fashion way, he inherited Conquest from his ancestors. He has a vendetta against old man Maywell who stole the company away from his grandfather. He blames his grandfather's death on old man Maywell, every since he has vowed to get even. But he was looking for an opportunity. The opportunity came knocking on his door when Maywell ousted Ty Dannerman as their CEO. Ty and Artie formed a partnership to literally destroy Maywell. Mr. Dannerman is responsible for stealing inside information from Maywell and passing it on to Conquest while setting up a global spy network to sell Maywell's software on the black market. This is why Maywell lost those contracts to Conquest. The grand jury in London had been investigating these spy networks along with the death of your colleague for some time, but hasn't come up with enough conclusive evidence to prosecute anyone because they all end up dead, "said the man.

"What is your part in all this," said Nicole.

"Well I was on Art's payroll until he and Ty tried to swindle me out of my share of the pie. I threatened to blow the whistle on them. I took evidence that could put them away for a very long time. If I have to go down, then I'm taking them bastards down with me. I had to go into hiding because they wanted to kill me like they did the other informant that talked to your colleague. The other informant informed me to talk to your colleague before they took him out. Your colleague was killed because they felt he had the goods on them. You and him were close wasn't you?" said the man.

"You tell me since you seemed to know everything," said Nicole.

"I don't need this attitude lady, do you want me to help you or not lady? my time is valuable," said the man.

"You got my attention," Nicole shouted as she looked over her shoulders.

"Be quiet lady! Keep it down; do you want to draw attention? said the man. Anyway, as I was saying before you rudely interrupt me, the other informant gave me the information that he allegedly gave to your colleague who indicated if something was to happen to him, which it did to contact you. So I'm following orders," said the man.

"So Aaron gave you my name," asked Nicole.

"The man knew you and your colleague were good friends so it was a no brainer that I pass that information on to you," said the man.

"You taken an awful big chance by meeting me here aren't you? How I know you won't turn on me like you turned on Ty and Art?" said Nicole.

"Yeah I am taking a chance, but you don't have a choice do you lady?" said the man.

"Yes I do, I can walk right out that door because I know you not doing this out of the goodness of your own heart. What's in it for you? Why do you want to help me? I know your conscience is not bothering you. You people don't have one," said Nicole.

"What do you mean by you people? Lady, please do not get smug with me. I'm a respectable businessman. I don't have time for all these questions. Don't you want me to help you or not," said the man.

"How do I know if you are telling me the truth? This could be some sort of trap," said Nicole.

"The point is you don't. You will have to trust me. You haven't been able to figure out all the funny business that has been happening with your company or the death of your colleague so far has you?" said the man.

Nicole knew right then the man had a point. After all, what he was saying seemed to make sense not to mention explaining what has been happening at Maywell. Plus, she definitely wanted to find out who was behind the death of Aaron. So she listens attentively to the man and let him finish what he had to say.

"Ty is a shyster in every since of the word. He would sell his soul to the devil. He has an ego bigger then the state of Texas. He is a despicable human being. He will do anything for the all mighty dollar," said the man.

"That's an understatement," said Nicole.

"Maywell board members grew tried of Ty's antics and decided to oust him as Maywell's CEO. He decided to fight back and threaten to sue the company for defamation of character. Plus, he had some dirt on the company, that Maywell was during business with some shady organizations run by some powerful people, all master minded by him, inflating Maywell's books with questionable loans. Making the company seem more profitable, plus he had assembled a dream team of attorneys to fight his legal battles with the company. Didn't you find it strange that Maywell would keep him around after they had canned his ass? That normally doesn't happen especially in this day and age. So the board decided to cut a deal with him to keep him on board to avoid public scrutiny. They gave him a huge settlement, which Ty called hush money. Ty agreed to give a public statement that he was stepping down as Maywell's CEO to be relieved of some of his duties due to personal reasons. But company officials were totally against it. They wanted the dust to settle," said the man.

Nicole never thought to ask anyone at Maywell why Ty was still employed at the company. She just thought he voluntarily stepped down. Plus, Maywell had the don't ask don't tell rule, but she did think it was out of character that board members still wanted him around.

The man continued on.

"Still fumed about the ouster, Ty struck a deal with Mr. McRand to destroy Maywell. And the stage was set. Ty knew Art had it in for Maywell because he knew Art detested Maywell more then he did. Mr. McRand poured money into Ty's pocket. They begun setting up dummy corporations. Money laundering, racketeering, they were running money through bogus accounts faster than Exlax runs through a person's system, they set-up Swiss bank accounts. Art is a man who hides behind his religious beliefs, a damn hypocrite. Ty hated you for taking his place. He would have hated anybody that came after him, but he totally despised you because of who you are, a woman. That was a total embarrassment to him to be replaced by a woman. He was the laughing stock of the industry. You came along at the wrong time. He wanted to belittle you, to put you in your place and make you look bad in front of the board members, hell in front of the world. He wanted to totally discredit you because he felt strongly you were all beauty and no brains," said the man.

"I knew it was something about that creep that didn't sit well with me. He tried to make me feel uncomfortable on purpose, the way he undresses me with his eyes," said Nicole.

"Ty is a womanizer, a damn freak if you ask me. And by you being a looker I'm sure he had his reasons for looking at you in that way, Nicole its up to you to nail those creeps. I've got to lay low; my life is depending on it. They have got me on the run. I will do my best to keep in contact with you, but for the most part I wash my hands with it. Don't call me, I will call you," said the man.

Nicole hoping the man would give her concrete proof so she could go straight to the authorities. She knew you couldn't count on a low life like this creep. These types of people are only in it to get their palms greased, the hell with anybody else. They will turn on you quicker then a heartbeat or sell you out to the highest bidder, but she had to admit that the man did shed some light on the situation.

Nicole went outside the pub and caught a cab. It was late and pouring down raining. On the way back to the hotel she was so angry that she could literally strangle Ty with her bare hands, that lowdown son of a bitch. She didn't care about losing out on the deals in fear of losing her job. At this point she didn't give a damn about a job.

Jobs come and go. The sad thing about all of this is that one of her closest friends is dead. All due to a low life like Ty Dannerman.

The next morning the London tabloid headline read, *Unidentified Man Found Shot to Death by an Apparent Drive-By*. Nicole saw her life pass right before her eyes. Immediately she knew she was in a fight for her life and dealing with some pretty shady and powerful characters. She needed help and she needed it fast.

CHAPTER 23

The President kept true to his word and passed legislation concerning MIA's who fought in the Vietnam War. The President passed a bill to generate funds to help families who lost love ones in the war. He appointed a special counsel to show interest in MIA's claims. There were thousands of people killed during the war.

The President didn't want the families to suffer any longer. His heart went out to these people. This counsel would investigate everything from dog tags, medical records to recent evidence found concerning MIA cases. All of this was due to the recent trade embargo lifted on North and South Korea.

The counsel spokesperson, Sheila Adair wanted to obtain any information that had been collected and sent to the National Defense Medical Center for testing. She informed the public that she would leave no stone unturned and promised to cut through the red tape in most of these cases. She informed the families of MIA's to be patient because help is on the way. That was music to the family's ears of MIA's even though they knew any information found would have to go through the POW and MIA offices first because claims must be documented first in order to proceed on with the investigations. Still it seemed like something was finally being done.

Ms. Adair indicated that the Department of Defense was cooperating with North and South Korean officials to aid in the search. She strongly reemphasized the word patience. The President appointed civil rights activist, Reverend Jess Caleb as an Ambassador to Vietnam in which the Senate overwhelmingly approved. He was also a Vietnam Veteran. Mr. Caleb had been a minister for some twenty years counseling families who had lost love ones in the Vietnam War. His congregation had raised millions of dollars through the years to help these families because they simply weren't getting enough financial assistance from the government. Some of these families were in a financially handicapped situation, to the point some were even homeless. Mr. Caleb had shelters for these people. So it was a no brainer that the President named him as the ambassador. Reverend Caleb had been on the battle lines of the civil rights movement. He was a person who didn't mind dying. His perception of death was to bring it on and face it like a man. He once stated that "dying was another form of moving on, a change of clothes." He also was quoted as saying "that if he could make it through the Vietnam War he could make it through any situation he is confronted with and he welcomed death."

Reverend Calab had won many awards through the years for his contributions he had made towards mankind. Humanitarian degrees from places like Harvard and so on, none of which he cared about because he felt that was what he was suppose to do. That's the whole duty of man. His mission in life was to help the less fortunate and he did that with every fiber of his being. He had dedicated over half of his life to fulfill that mission.

Reverend Caleb was in Ho Chi Minh City searching records at the MIA office when he made an amazing discovery. There were cases where MIA's had survived the war and some setup shop in Southeast Asia that had been missing since the Vietnam War living under assumed names. Many had remarried and started families. Most of them had lost their memories and had no recollection of ever fighting in the war. This condition was called post-traumatic stress disorder.

Reverend Caleb was informed that a doctor in Ho Chi Minh City had been treating MIA's for this condition using natural resources along with experimental drugs in some cases.

CHAPTER 24

As she returned to the States the only thing Nicole could think about was how she would possibly keep a working relationship with Ty let alone maintaining her composure while she is around him. She never felt comfortable around him from day one because she always got an uneasy feeling. When she looked into his eyes it was though they were dead, like nothing was there. She felt the bastard needed to be executed for the crimes he had committed. She had heard people in the office accuse Ty of many devious deeds, but never in a million years would she have thought he was a murderer.

She was confused as hell, didn't know which way to turn. She never thought she would be caught in the middle of a game of espionage. She felt this was the type of stuff you read about in novels or see on a Perry Mason flick. Nicole felt as though she was about to lose her mind. But what should she do?

· · · · · · · · ·

It was business as usual at the office. Nicole knew she must act normal, but she wondered how.

"Nicole how was your trip?" her secretary asked.

"Business as usual under the circumstances," said Nicole.

"That's right you went to London to tie up some loose ends as far as Aaron was concern. He was a nice man. It seems like the good people on this earth always seems to die first," said her secretary.

Nicole knew her secretary was just making conversation. It's situations like these a person doesn't know what to say. Hell, they all were suffering because of Aaron's death.

Nicole was fuming, but kept her composure. Her secretary was right, people like Aaron always seems to die first, especially in this case. If anyone deserves to die it should have been Ty.

"Life and death are issues beyond our control." said Nicole.

"Nicole, are you sure you are ready to come back to work so soon? I know how close you and Aaron were," said her secretary.

"All things considered I have no choice. I have too many things on my plate. So much work needed to be done while emotions are running high. I have to name a replacement for Aaron, but until I do I must follow through on Aaron's behalf. He did such a marvelous job and replacing him is going to be one of the most difficult things I'll have to do. He was on top of the situation. The man left no stones unturned. I had the utmost confidence in him. He knew the market like the backside of his hand. Not to mention what he done with Sparcomat, it's beyond my wildest expectations. He literally carried the company on his shoulders doing the difficult times, especially when lost out on those deals. Sparcomat was our cash cow. The revenue Sparomat generated saved our Asses because all of us would have been at Kinko's making copies of our resume if you get my drift," said Nicole.

Nicole had a person in mind to replace Aaron, that person was none other than James in marketing. James was a prodigy of Aaron. Nicole felt that James had paid his dues and should be rewarded for his expertise.

One of those things on Nicole's plate was to bring Ty down. That's her first agenda. As far as she was concerned Maywell could go to hell at this particular point and time. This was personal and vengeance would be hers this time around. She was going to help the man upstairs this time around just in case he might be to busy. She has to fight fire with fire. She would ask the man upstairs for forgiveness because she knew she had to reap what she sows. Never in a million years; she thought, would she ever feel this way. She just felt bitter and that's putting it mildly. The hostility in her had reached its boiling point. She has been upset since Robert's death, now Aaron has died. Aaron was like a big brother to her. A brother she never had. Her heart went out to his family. She found it hard to believe that a man literally got himself killed for during his job. Somehow she felt responsible because if she had never named Aaron to spearhead operation Europe then this probably would have never happened, even though bad blood existed between him and Ty. "What is the world coming to," she thought to herself. She tried hard to do some work, but she wasn't productive. The walls of the office seemed like they were closing in on her. When she thought about Aaron she had to fight back the tears, then afterwards she got angry. This went on and on for a period of time. She was getting fidgety, tossing in turning in her chair, chewing the tip of her pen as though she was trying to drain all the ink out it. It was a good thing Ty was out of town because if he had showed up at the office today she would catch a case, a murder in the first degree as a matter of fact.

By the time she looked at her watch nearly everyone at the office had gone home. It was late. It was dark and rainy. The effects of hurricane June had reached havoc off the Carolina coast with winds gusting at a hundred and twenty miles per hour destroying everything in its path. The national weather service informed every one to seek shelter. All businesses along the coast were boarded up, it looks like a ghost town down the eastern seaboard.

Nicole took off for home. The roads were slick, but she had to stop and get some gas. Once at home she went over and over Aaron's diary for the umpteenth time. She still couldn't make sense of much of the information that Aaron had written in code. The question was how? How does she break through these codes? Who could she turn to? Questions after questions, but dam it she need answers. These codes could be the proof she needed to nail that bastard to the wall. Immediately she remembered one of the names of an engineer who worked with Aaron on Sparcomat. She felt he could provide her with enough adequate technical support to break through these codes. She gives him a call. She didn't go into an in depth conversation of what she wanted. He informed Nicole, step by step of what she needed to do on her computer in order to read the codes. The system engineer told Nicole about the system they used with Sparomat. Nicole had some of the software Aaron used with Sparcomat. Nicole was comfortable with her computer's capabilities all she had to do was to be patient, but time was running out. She wanted to break through these codes like yesterday. She had a good working knowledge of Sparcomat, Aaron was very secretive when it came to his work. He didn't want the information to fall in the wrong hands.

The engineer informed Nicole that breaking the codes was a piece of cake all she had to do was to go online and log on www.sparcomat.com/features and click on programs and it will walk her through the process. Aaron had set-up the codes to references the material. Nicole transferred the information on another disc because other people at Maywell may have access to the information. Sparcomat allowed people to log on and take classes all over the world through e-learning. A person could take the same class whether they are in England, Japan or the United States, it didn't matter. Nicole felt the timing was right to include North and South Korea because e-learning will be the wave or the method of teaching by the next millennium.

CHAPTER
25

Since Aaron's death, things haven't been the same at the company. "The show must go on," a Maywell spokesman told the media. He wasn't being insensitive, just factual. Even though things were somber at headquarters Maywell did receive some good news. It was nominated and received a reward for being the top computer service company for the fifth year in a row. This was because they matched their competitor's price. Shareholders were quite pleased, but they still were looking at the overall picture.

At the board meeting Nicole was watching Ty's every move. She felt Ty was a sheep in wolf's clothing, which is leading Maywell astray, to the slaughter nevertheless. Nicole managed to keep her composure as she was discussing Maywell's projected figures for the next quarter. She felt as though she deserved an academy award for acting calm a not exposing Ty for the creep that he is. This was hard, staring down the face of a murderer. Something in her couldn't take it anymore as she excused herself from the meeting and went to the lady's room. Once in the lady's room she felt she needed to throw up. Looking at Ty made her sick in the stomach. She put some cold water on her face. She looked in the mirror and felt she had aged. She felt as though this job, the pressure at least would send her to an early grave.

Back at the meeting, board members were brainstorming on how to get Maywell back on track, mainly naming a replacement. Nicole indicated to the board that James in marketing should be the one to replace Aaron. The board overwhelmingly approved.

Ty indicated that maybe Maywell needed to hire counselors to help employees with their grief and to improve their morale. "Isn't this some shit," Nicole thought to herself? First of all, this is not some high school trying to help an adolescence cope with their grief. This is a place of business. This SOB got the nerve to try to smooth over a situation he created. No one would be grieving if it weren't for his ass. How could he let that even roll off his lips, but he was good, very good. That's one of the characteristics of the devil to charm people in order to draw attention away from him self. Nicole felt Ty was Satan in a body. She'd had enough and started to blurt out to the rest of the board members that Ty was responsible for all this mayhem at the company, but soon came to her senses because she didn't have enough proof plus her life would be in danger.

Ty was telling some of the board members that he might take a few days off to go play golf. Just to get away from the office for a little while. This was perfect timing on his part. The real reason he wanted to get away was to plot his next move. It seemed like everything was going his way and once his mission was complete he could ride away in the sunset with his millions and live happy every after. He felt justice would have prevailed once he sees that great bastion, Maywell crumble like a cookie.

Ty flew down to St. Croix. The hurricane season just had ended which almost destroyed the island. The people there on the island did a wonderful job of cleaning up the place after the catastrophe. Tourist was everywhere, roaming the beach. The beach houses were completely occupied. St. Croix was beautiful this time of year. The pretty blue waters of the island would take your breath away. The weather was beautiful, not a cloud in the sky. The people on the beach were doing their thing. Some playing games while others were just relaxing in the sun.

Ty was lying on the beach sipping on a drink when a man approached him wearing dark sunglasses.

"What's the word," said Ty.

"Word has it that Nicole was at the pub the same night the informant was there," said the man.

"Did anyone see them together at anytime at the pub," said Ty.

"I assume, well I really don't know," said the man.

"What do you mean, you really don't know. You are paid to know these things, we can't assume a damn thing," Ty shouted.

"The setting was dark in the pub. An it probably was a mere coincidence that they were there at the same time," said the man.

"I don't give a damn if it was dark or not. I can't afford to take that chance. Knowing Nicole like I do, nothing is a mere coincidence. That broad leaves nothing to chance," said Ty.

"Well the informant got waxed after we finally track him down. So why does it matter," said the man.

"Are you that stupid. The SOB could have been meeting her there to give her some valuable information concerning our operation. Dam it I told Art the less people involved the better off we would be. If you want something done right dam it you have to do it yourself," said Ty.

"Well I have done what I suppose to do. Where is my money?" said the man.

Ty reached down in his bag a pulled out an envelope and handed it to the man. The man looked in the envelope and counted the money and looked up at Ty in surprise.

"This is not the amount that we agreed upon. When do I get the other half of my money," said the man.

"I don't know," said Ty.

"What do you mean you don't know," said the man.

"Like you told me you don't know if the informant and Nicole talked. I don't know when you will get the other half of your money," said Ty.

"Why you SOB, trying to stiff me out of my share," said the man.

"You lucky you got that much for the shitty job you done, you don't deserve that much. You lucky you didn't get what the informant got. You know what I mean. Now get out of face before you become a shark's meal or be found by some old man fishing," said Ty.

The man was angry as he vowed to get even. Even though he knew Ty didn't make idle threats. He didn't seem to care if his life was in danger or not. "I want my damn money," he shouted as he walked away. Ty burst into laughter, but at the same time was mad as hell.

The wind was breezy as Nicole went on an early morning jog. Nicole was back at Martha's Vineyard for a short sabbatical to decide her next move. Nicole jogged along the beach where tourist hung out as seagulls surrounded the famous lighthouse. Edgartown, Massachusetts seemed a world apart, but not far enough. No place on this earth would be far enough to escape the tragedies that have transpired in her life. When she arrived she was mentally and physically tired. She was emotionally drained to be exact. Aaron's death still haunted her till this day. It seemed like the men she cared about somehow always managed to die an early and senseless death. After Robert's death she felt empty inside and hoped she would never experience that feeling ever again. Even though Aaron was a friend that feeling had returned.

After her jog, she returned to her renovated beach house. The contractors had done an excellent job in renovating the house. They replaced some of the wood on the house, which needed repairs because of the sea salt from the ocean. They had painted the exterior and interior of the house. Thank goodness the fumes had dissipated. The biggest changes were in the kitchen where a wet bar was installed along with an island. Nicole had a Jacuzzi installed in her bedroom. A sauna was installed at the left wing of the beach house. These types of renovations were highly unusual for a beach house, but Nicole was an innovator in the boardroom and at home.

Nicole was very pleased with the renovations, which served somewhat as a distraction from her recent troubles. She thought time and time again of what her mother use to always tell her, "that troubles don't last always." She has had a tough time of it lately. Like she had fallen and couldn't get up.

Wilma, Nicole's maid has a key to the place and comes by twice a week to cleanup. Wilma always knew when Nicole was coming to town. She would always stock the refrigerator with Nicole's favorite foods. Wilma was just like a mom to Nicole and Nicole loved her dearly and trusted her with her life.

She sat on the balcony with her feet propped up looking at the ocean while sorting through her mail. She ran across a vacation package concerning a trip to Monte Carlo-Monaco, cruising down the Italian Riviera. It sounded sensational; she could picture herself already there, enjoying the festivities. Monaco is a glamorous place with a worldwide reputation, but pictures of Ty kept dancing in her head, which ruined the moment. She felt she had to put a stop to all of this madness once in for all. She looked up at a seagull and wondered why life can't be that simple for humans, living fancy frees, no troubles, not being bound. Then she looked down at the beach and saw tourist walking along the beach some holding hands, being romantic, then realized love is a beautiful thing. Man has an awesome responsibility in this creation she felt bearing all kinds of burdens.

It was early Sunday morning and Nicole neighbors knew she was in town thanks to Wilma. They stopped by and asked Nicole if she wanted to attend early morning service with them at Union Chapel, a nondenominational church in Oak Bluff that was built in the late 1800's. The chapel was a local favorite for tourist especially for those who wanted to get married. Nicole kindly declined their offer. She wanted to stay home to meditate in order to cleanse her soul. She needed some answers or a personal revelation to understand what she has been going through lately. Maybe this is why all this happen in the first place because she has turned her back on her religious beliefs or faith as she called it. Not intentionally, but she has been so engulfed with corporate and personal matters that she didn't have time to think about spiritual matters. When Robert died she was caught in a pickle, not nothing what or who to believe in. She was so angry she felt she lost faith and nothing about religion made any sense, especially the organizations she had been associated with. She just felt all she had to do was believe, but in what? She didn't have a clue.

It was noon and Nicole went to Vineyard Haven to have lunch at the Black Day Tavern. The people were friendly and glad to see her back on the island. It was one of Robert's favorite places along with Farm Neck Golf Club when they visited the island. Robert was teaching her how to play golf before he went to Vietnam. She felt golf was an interesting game, a good way to relieve stress. She played sparingly. It felt great to get out.

She went back to the beach house to play with some figures on the computer. She combed through some memos and other important documents. She briefly looked at the disc she copied concerning Aaron's diary searching for clues.

It was dinnertime and Nicole met some friends at Linda Jones's restaurant on Oak Bluff for dinner. They all chatted about old times and life's little hidden mysteries.

It was a beautiful night; the temperature had dropped a little. The reflection of the full moon made the ocean look like mingle glass, a perfect night for lovers that would put anyone in the mood for love. Nicole walked along the beach while feeling Robert's presence very near.

The next morning in her office Nicole was reading in the Wall Street Journal about Conquest lavish party that had all the usual trimmings due to the success of a strong second quarter. Their PC sales were far above industry expectations. Conquest CEO, Art McRand was the hit of the party because he passed out profit sharing checks to all company employees. Top industry analysts along with some local and state politicians were in attendance. Politicians were hanging around like blood flowing in shark-infested waters, hoping to receive a contribution to their re-election campaign. Mr. McRand invited his friends as he called them to the party so that Conquest could have influence over some local and state issues down the road. Conquest already has huge dealing with the state government. Politicians literally had their hands in their pockets to solicit big money for their special interest groups. He felt big business and politics go hand and hand so each side can promote their agendas. McRand's motto was never bite the hand that feed you. You scratch my back and I scratch yours. You can have your cake and it too if you play your cards right. He believed in the power of the pen. Art didn't give a damn about soft or hard money when it came to campaign finance reforms.

Nicole felt differently, she tried her level best to steer Maywell away from the political arena in making campaign contributions to political candidates because the two just don't mix, if Maywell employees wanted to make personal campaign contributions that was their business. Corporate contributions endorsing political candidates make strange bedfellows. It could come back to haunt you, just ask some of the companies that have been hit with some of the biggest lawsuits. They eventually stepped on someone toes. Plus, it causes trouble down the line and taxpayers ultimately will be the big losers. But people like Ty and Art don't care about the little guys, the customers, and the small business people striving to make it. Money is their friend and that's all that matters. Ty's motto was that people disappoint you, money don't.

Nicole felt that greed would be Ty's downfall. He will become careless and when he does she will nail his ass to the wall. It may take weeks or maybe a month or longer who knows, she will be waiting on him because a fool and his money do error in his ways.

"Yeah, she shouted within herself, maybe that's a plan," Sit back and wait and let Ty tie his own noose around his neck and hang him self. Then again she didn't want to sit around and do nothing because the future of Maywell depended upon it. She's running against the clock. She couldn't sniff around and ask questions because Ty might be on to her. One of the hardest things she would have to do is try to act normal around him. Hell, she was use to Ty stares, which she ignored. She felt they were stares of admiration and lust. He was just being a normal man. She felt most women would handle it differently and welcome Ty advances just to weaken him and have him foaming at the mouth. But the thought of Ty coming on to her would make her vomit.

She had all of Aaron's documents she brought back from London. Thank goodness Ty didn't get his hands on them first, which was his first mistake. He already had the man killed because he felt he knew too much. Nicole needed clues and if she has to go through all Aaron's documents to find them she would. She didn't want to leave nothing to chance. If she would have to make copies of all his records she would because she didn't know what exactly she was looking for. Finding the time would be the problem. She needed some help to sort through this chaos, but the less people involved the better, she had to keep reminding herself. Damn she wished Robert were alive. She knew she could count on him. He was so analytical and resourceful. Plus, it would have been nice if they could have faced this together. It would have been hard trying to keep it from him and not getting him involved.

She put her head down on her desk as though she praying, thinking of what could she do to handle this matter quickly and resourcefully. She has been through this before. It seems every time she sits at her desk she couldn't get any work done. Her mind keeps wondering. And it's not helping looking at Art's face plastered on the front page of the Wall Street Journal. She could literally smack that smug look off his face. There she goes again threatening to do bodily harm to someone. Before this stuff started with Ty and Art, the thought never would have entered her mind of laying her hands on someone to do them bodily harm. But this is the person she had become. She personally didn't like it because it was very tiring. She made a promise to herself that tonight will be the night she would come up with a plan; first she would have to start sifting through Aaron's documents. A voice said to her, "no exceptions Nicole, and no exceptions!!!" Since this whole ordeal started she noticed a pattern had developed. It seemed as though she was constantly repeating herself, saying the same thing over and over again, talking to herself more frequently. "Damn I'm I losing my damn mind?"

CHAPTER 28

Reverend Caleb following an anonymous tip was introduced to Dr. Cho Sing, a leading psychiatrist in Vietnam, who treated war veterans suffering from severe post-traumatic stress disorder caused by the Vietnam War. Dr. Sing had done extensive research in the field of psychiatry concerning this condition. His therapy included making the person who is afflicted with this condition come face to face with that traumatic experience.

"Hi, Dr. Sing I'm Rev. Caleb, the ambassador to Vietnam from the United States."

"Nice to meet you Sir," said Dr. Sing.

"I'm here on a mission of trying to gather data, facts, or whatever information possible on finding MIA's or POW's that fought in the Vietnam War. I have spent countless hours in gathering and sorting through data compiled in these cases trying to locate records, evidence or something to put some closure to the matter so their love ones back home can finally have peace of mind. Can you help me with this matter?"

"I'll do what I can. What do you need from me," said the doctor?

"First and foremost could you tell me a little about your methods, your methods of treatment in helping MIA's and POW's? I know I'm reaching, but how far I don't know. Just tell me something that may enlighten me in your area of study, "said the Reverend.

"Sure, I understand a man in your position. Basically what I do is make my patient comes to grips with the trauma that caused the disorder. I do not press because that can backfire on you. I try to jog their memory. Make them think about something good that has transpired in their life. I do little exercises like show and tell. What I mean by this is that I show them something and they tell me what it means to them. Something like, a picture which proves to be the most effective. Sometimes their memory snaps back in an instance by using this method, mind over matter. The brain is a powerful machine. I hardly ever use medication unless it's a severe case because some of the chemicals used in the war reached havoc on their health. Those chemicals were so subtle it can be deadly if the condition goes untreated. No one really knows the effect the chemicals really had on the body. I know it sounds like a direct contradiction, but it the truth. Most of the time medication makes the situation worst and I don't want to over medicate them. The brain is a funny thing, "said the doctor.

"Doc all I know is when it comes to the brain I know very little. Funny you mention medication though. Can the brain, I'm talking about human behavior be treated with medication like other organs in the body, "said the Reverend.

"Some doctors will say yes, but I personally don't believe in it. You said it earlier, years ago people knew very little about the brain as for as treating it, but as time has progressed, researchers have discovered that the brain can be treated like any other organ in his body. The brain has the ability to heal itself because the cells constantly regenerate. That's always been my theory," said the doctor.

"Doc what are some of the symptoms of post traumatic stress disorder."

"Rage is one of them, trying to let go of that bad experience. It's like that experience is eating away at them little by little, a leaky water hydrant that keeps dripping on the concrete. Over a period of time the concrete turns dark and eventually cracks. That's how the mind works. You put too much pressure on it, it will eventually crack," said the doctor.

"Yeah tell be about it. I think the hardest part for Vietnam Veterans is being accepted back into the mainstream. That's where I come in; the American Legion has done a marvelous job in making sure Vietnam Veterans rights are preserved. Some of the veterans are treated harshly by society," said the Reverend.

"When you are dealing with the exploration of one's psyche that's enough said right there. But having society to treat them differently is a traumatic experience within itself," said the doctor.

"That's the point I'm trying to make. To bridge the gap between these people and make them productive citizens again so they want be discriminated against. Wait doc let me show you something," said the Reverend.

While digging through his briefcase, a picture of Robert fell on the floor and before he could pick it up the doctor bent over and pick it up first as though he had seen a ghost. The Reverend got Robert picture from senator Gatewood. Robert case was a high priority. Some top politicians like senator Gatewood and senator Thread; even the President was pressing the issue to put some closure on the matter for Nicole sake.

"What's wrong doc? Do you know this man," said the Reverend?

"Yeah I treated him, a POW. He was an unusual patient. He had a strong amount of determination, but also he had a severe case of post- traumatic stress disorder, "said the doctor.

"What happen to him," said the Reverend?

"I don't know. I wished I knew. He just disappeared into thin so it seems. He was one of my model patients. I wanted to use him as a testimonial for the other patients. He booked a follow-up appointment and never showed up, "said the doctor.

"I be darned," said the Reverend as something else almost slipped out of his mouth, but being a man of the cloth he caught himself.

By this time a patient came in to see Dr. Sing as they were looking at Robert's picture.

"Hi doc, I'm here for my appointment, "said the patient.

The patient didn't speak good English so the doctor had to translate his conversation in English for the Reverend to understand and visa versa.

"I'll be right with you, "said the good doctor.

"Doc, what's with the concern look," said the patient.

"We were looking at this picture of a former patient of mine and wondering what happen to him. It just seems he disappeared into thin air or off the face of the earth so it seems," said the doctor.

"Let me take a look. Oh! That's Ben, "said the man.

"What you call him," said the Reverend.

"Ben," said the man.

"His name, his name is Robert, do you know him? Do you know his whereabouts?" said the Reverend.

"I don't know him, but I know of him. He lives right outside the city in a village with his family. Everybody just called him Ben," said the patient.

"Can you take me to him, "said the Reverend.

"Sure first thing in the morning. Meet me back here at the doctor's office at 10:00 a.m.," said the man.

It was getting late and the Reverend headed back to the hotel. "This is unusual," he thought to himself that a POW can still be alive after all these years, but stranger things have happened. He noticed the man said Robert lived with his family. Could this man be Robert or a case of mistaken identity?" The Reverend mind was racing with questions. It's still hard to believe because these POW's were made to serve with rigor. Some of these POW's were coerced, terrorized, and even assassinated over the years; as some of these concentration camps were severely attacked. POW's were kidnapped and ambushed during this regime. "No he can't be alive unless he had a strong will to live. Calm down Reverend and just pray about it," a voice within him said. Then he begins to wonder was this a hoax. One thing for sure he wasn't going to get his hopes up. Until he actually sees Robert for himself then he would believe. He knew this would be a sleepless night.

The next morning the Reverend met the young gentleman at the doctor's office at precisely 10:00 a.m, like he said. The Reverend felt that was a good sign, the guy actually showed up when he said he would. At least he was a man of his word. It was kind of a long journey to the village, but the Reverend didn't mind. He had come this far it was no way in the world he was going to turn back now. He had always preached to his congregation that success is a journey, not a destination. As they approached the village they walked up to the place where Robert was staying. Robert wasn't there. No one wanted to answer any questions as they looked at one another as though they were hiding something. Then low and behold Robert walked up. Immediately Reverend Caleb knew that this wasn't a dream. He said a prayer from within, a prayer of thanks because his prayer had been answered. He believed in predestination, the power of faith.

They introduced themselves and Robert followed them back to Dr. Sing's office. As they were going back to the doctor's office all the good Reverend could think about was that miracles do happen everyday. He also thought about using this ordeal as a testimonial for a future sermon.

Reverend Caleb had a picture of Nicole and before he showed it to Robert, Robert was explaining what actually happen. His plane was shot down, he was captured by the enemy and spitefully treated, went for days without food and water. One night the camp was ambushed, but he found favor with this particular woman named Minah who took care of him and nursed him back into good health. Minah eventually fell in love with him, who spared his life by hiding him for three months. Minah took him food and clothing nursed his wounds all under one condition that he never forsakes her. Robert admitted he loved Minah, but not in a way a man should love a woman. The relationship was strictly platonic. He remained faithful only because he told Minah he suffered severe nerve damage and couldn't have a sexual relationship with her. Robert knew he loved someone dearly in a past life, but couldn't remember who, which kept him faithful. He took care of her and her three kids she had by her husband who was killed in the war. Robert said Minah had severe health problems and eventually died and he just couldn't leave her after she took good care of him. He promised her he would take care of the kids and know the time has come that he had fulfilled her wishes and it was time to move on. He was a man of his word.

At this time the Reverend showed Robert a picture of Nicole and immediately he remembered the life they shared together. It was though he was shocked back into reality. Nicole was his enter strength that kept him alive. Robert was in great shape. He told Reverend Caleb that he was ready to head back to the States because he had fulfilled his promised to Minah. He was sure Nicole would understand. Robert and the Reverend headed back home.

CHAPTER
29

It was the holiday season and Maywell finished with a strong third quarter, not to their expectations but overall it was pretty decent. Conquest was much better. Maywell had spent millions of dollars in advertising for the big holiday push on their new PC's. Their archrival, Conquest had stolen some of their thunder once again because their PC's was put on the market before Maywell's. Maywell wasn't intimidating giant it once was and Conquest had overtaken them in some areas of the industry. This was not surprising to Nicole because she knew Conquest was committing highway robbery with Ty being the main culprit.

Conquest Christmas party at the Trump Towers was nothing short of spectacular with all their employees once again received lavish gifts and hefty bonuses for all their hard work. Both companies were engaged in an all out war to finish the year on a strong note because the economy the previous year had been dismal to say the least.

As far as Nicole was concerned, this was secondary. The hell with forecasting and budgets, she fully understood why Conquest had out performed Maywell lately. Her primary focus these days was finding enough evidence to connect Ty with Aaron's death. The informant failed to give her conclusive evidence concerning this matter that would link Ty to the murder. London authorities were still gathering evidence surrounding the case. Nicole didn't want to tip off London authorities because she didn't have enough evidence, but more importantly she didn't want Ty and his cronies on to her. She figured he knew she was on to him just by the way he had been acting of late.

Ty felt Nicole was acting strange so he wanted very much to teach her a lesson so she wouldn't get any ideas of trying to play hero. Ty didn't know what Nicole knew, but he figured she knew something and he wanted to eliminate all potential problems. He and Art knew that Nicole met with the informant. He had all of Nicole's systems bugged and wanted to monitor her comings and goings.

·········

Every holiday season Nicole and Robert use to spend the holidays together at Martha's Vineyard. Christmas wouldn't be Christmas if she didn't spend the holidays there. Local forecasters had predicted a white Christmas. The rain and the snow had buried the New England leaves that had fallen in the fall. People from all over the country came to this part of the country each year during this time just to see Mother Nature at its finest.

Nicole unpacked, called her mother to let her know she made it there safely and wish her a Merry Christmas. Her mother usually spends the holiday season with her there since Robert's death, but this particular time her mother decided to go on a cruise with some of bridge club friends. Her mother didn't want to go because this time of the year is made to be around family, but Nicole insisted that she go. Nicole loved her mother, but under the circumstances, she wanted to be by herself this particular holiday season because of the things she had to deal with.

Nicole gathered at the club with some of her friends there on the island, both senator Gatewood and senator Thread were accompanied by their wives along some other prominent people that usually spend their holiday season at the Vineyard. It was during this time of the year that Nicole had a hard time coming to grips with Robert's death because he always made the holidays seemed so special. They would take romantic walks, hand and hand along the ocean, pick out the brightest star and make a wish, come back to the beach house and share stories and cuddle up around the fireplace while drinking hot apple cider and eggnog until they get all tingly inside. They would get-up the next morning and open their gifts. Christmas was all about sharing and this time she had no one to share it with, not even her mother. It was nice the senators invited her to spend time with them and their families. She didn't want to feel like a third wheel because she felt married people don't usually invite single people, especially women to gathering such as this because of jealousy reasons. Under the circumstances, she still managed to have a great time being amongst friends. They all exchanged stories, most of them were just fables to get a laugh or two. It was getting late and they all said their goodbyes. Nicole went back to the beach house got her some hot apple cider and was going through Aaron's dairy in front of the fireplace until she fell asleep. She had made some head way since talking with the engineer.

The next morning, she opened the door for some fresh air and there on the front porch was a large box neatly wrapped in gift paper with no return address. The package was addressed to her. This brought a smile to her face as she picked-up the box. She knew it was from her mother wishing her a happy holiday season since she didn't make the trip with her this time. She felt a little guilty because she would have to wait and give her mother her gift after the holidays. When she opened the box and looked into it and she nearly fainted. In the box was a black chicken heart with dead roses. She dropped the box and at this time, she knew this wasn't a prank, but realized her life was in danger and that she was in a fight for her life. "Dam it Ty is on to me," she said to herself. She knew Ty was a coward and one of the characteristics of a coward was to intimidate.

Nicole was pressing hard to find concrete evidence, as she was reading Aaron's dairy she noticed a little compartment in the cover of the dairy. All this time she had the dairy she just now noticed it. She opened it and in it was a computer disc. Nicole put the disc in her computer, "bing-go," she shouted to herself, and to her surprise, the disc had all the information she had been looking for to nail that SOB, Ty to the wall along with his cronies. Nicole couldn't believe the information she needed was right under her nose all along that just so happen, just literally fell into her lap, the disc outline Ty and Art entire espionage attempt along with evidence of money laundering and evidence concerning Aaron's death. "How stupid could a person be," Nicole said to herself. Putting this kind of information on a disc, this could fall into the wrong hands. The smartest of criminals make mistakes and slip up from time to time, she figured Aaron got the disc from the informant who stole it from Ty that's why he got eliminated. Ty put the information on disc to cover his own behind because he didn't trust Art. Crooks don't trust crooks and it takes one to know one. Ty just overplayed his hands. Nicole figured once Ty settled the score he would use the evidence to incriminate Art and blame him for the whole ordeal because they didn't like one another. She knew Ty didn't give a damn about anyone except himself.

He used Art as the front man because when the ball drops Art will be the one left holding the bag.

Nicole was so overwhelmed about the information she had before her she stayed up until the wee hours of the morning going over and over the incriminating evidence. All kinds of questions were running through her mind. "Should she take the evidence straight to the board or to the authorities?" "Nah that would be to easy," she thought to herself. She wanted that SOB to suffer, but first she had to make copies of the disc to cover herself in the event they tried to eliminate her like they did Aaron. She figured Ty was looking for the disc. She knew she couldn't make the copies at work or at home in fear of the system being bugged.

Nicole decided to take the first flight back to Orangeburg the very next morning. Upon arrival in Orangeburg on a cold winter day, a snowstorm had blanketed the eastern seaboard. As soon as she stepped of the plane, Nicole went straight to kinko's to copy the disc. She would put them in a safe deposit box at the bank with instructions if something were to happen to her, the copies would be safely delivered to someone she trusted.

Ty was following Nicole and saw her going into kinko's and thought it was very strange that Nicole would go into a place like kinko's because whatever she needed done she could have easily had it done at the office. Ty went into kinko's and charmed the girl at the counter and she let on that Nicole had copies made off a disc. Ty knew that some discs were missing from Conquest office because the informant stole them and right away he knew Nicole was on to him. He ran out kinko's to his car, and called Art and told him Nicole was on to them.

· · · · · · · · ·

On Friday, New Year's Eve, Nicole and Maywell's board members, Ty included met at the club for a party to bring in the New Year with a bang. The party was a blast and some board members had to have designated drivers because some of them were blasted. Once Nicole got home she took a swim in the heated pool, showered and got dressed for bed. As she begins to fall asleep, she heard a noise, she immediately sat-up in the bed, but didn't hear anything further and fell off to sleep. Her bedroom door was shut, but unlocked. As she dosed off, a man entered her room and put his hand over her mouth and told her not to scream if she wanted to stay alive. The man told Nicole he would slice her throat into pieces if she even looks like she wanted to scream. The man tied Nicole's feet and hands together with duct tape. He carried Nicole down stairs.

The kidnapper along with another man who was waiting in a van loaded Nicole in the van. They had her wrapped up like a piece of carpet. They drove to an abandon warehouse in Myrtle Beach own by no other than Art McRand. Art had thought about moving Conquest headquarters to Myrtle Beach from Atlanta, just to piss off Maywell in order to be a good neighbor, to be in their own backyard.

Nicole was putting two and two together. Art holdings and investments were done through Conquest business accounts not his personal accounts as a write-off for tax purposes. Nicole didn't lose her composure; she was too mad. If she was going to die then let's get it over with, she had nothing to lose and made up her mind to go down fighting.

The plane touched down at Dulles Airport. It was a long flight; Robert was anxious to get back home to see his loved Nicole. Reverend Caleb had briefed Robert on what had been actually going on with the government inducement with MIA's and POW's, which fought in the war. Robert vowed to lend his support to such a great cause and personally thanked the Reverend for all the hard work he had done. Robert started to ask questions about Nicole and the Reverend went on to explain that Nicole had become one of the famous women/person in America and that she had dedicated his memory as a memorial to all Vietnam Veterans.

Reverend Caleb also informed Robert that Nicole had captured the hearts of man including the President's, which made his case a personal mission. While getting off the airplane, there were no parade or banners to welcome the fallen hero back on U.S. soil. Robert preferred it that way. He wanted no honor from men for serving his country. He felt his country owed him nothing and that he was the lucky one for having the chance to serve his country in honor. He was thrilled to death to have his feet back on U.S. soil.

Little did Robert know that Reverend Caleb had informed senator Gatewood and senator Thread that Robert was on the way home, they had set-up at a later date along with the President to give Robert a proclamation and a purple heart for his bravery during the war, the date was set-aside until the President returned from his peace mission from the Middle East with other world leaders.

Senators Gatewood and senator Thread were extremely glad to see Robert, especially senator Thread because he blamed himself for Robert's death. It was as if all the guilt he had bottled up inside just all of a sudden gone away. It was a relief off his shoulders, a monkey off his back. They both were in disbelief, but happy at the same time.

"Robert, you look better than any dead man I've seen alive," said senator Gatewood.

"Yeah the Vietnamese have this miracle ointment that kept me looking younger by the day," said Robert.

They all laughed as they were on their way to Capitol Hill.

"Talk about reincarnation," said senator Thread.

"You have to die in order to be reincarnated senator. I haven't gone anywhere yet," said Robert.

"Gentlemen this man was a real trooper that has more lives than a cat," said Reverend Caleb.

"It just wasn't my time that's all. I have a lot to live and be thankful for," said Robert.

"Yeah you got that right. You definitely have a guardian angel looking over you, that's for sure, "said senator Gatewood.

"Speaking of angels how is Nicole? I know you guys have played a major part in my return as well as keeping tabs on Nicole. I want to thank each one of you personally. There is no one more important to me in my life more than that woman "said Robert.

"Man I missed you," said senator Thread.

"Nicole has done an absolute marvelous job in juggling her career and personal life under the circumstances," said senator Gatewood.

They arrived on Capitol Hill, there was a late breaking story on the news that said "Maywell's CEO was missing." The details were sketchy, but stay tune for their local news. They all were in complete shock as they scrambled to get information concerning Nicole whereabouts.

....

A package arrived on John Aslong desk that was marked urgent, top secret. Mr. Aslong opened the package that had Nicole's name on it as the sender. In the package was the computer disc that Nicole had made copies of at kinko's. John popped the disc in his computer and saw the information concerning Ty's involvement in the espionage attempt to destroy Maywell.

He called an emergency board meeting along with local authorities to inform the board on the information he had received. They were all steamed under the collar, kicking them selves for letting that low life Ty make a fool of them. They knew he couldn't be trusted, but under the circumstances Ty hand their hands tied. They thought they were doing the right thing by keeping him on board at the time to avoid bad publicity to protect their own Asses.

"I be damn, we should have cut all ties with that son of a bitch when we canned his ass," said John Aslong.

"We should have said the hell with some damn bad publicity, took our chances. We walked around with our head in our asses walking on eggshells of what that SOB might do and we still got our asses burnt fooling around with that bastard. It could not be any worst now. We gambled and we lost big time," said Paul Monday.

"Dam it I knew it wasn't mere coincidence we lost out on those deals to Conquest. Those sorry ass bastards can't hold a candle to us," said board member Harold Comet.

All the board members had their say and were in total disbelief. There main concern was getting Nicole back save and sound.

Sure enough Ty had skipped town, cleaned out his office and his home. No one knew his whereabouts. All they knew was that he had vanished into thin air without a trace. They turned the information over to local authorities.

....

On a flight back to corporate headquarters in Atlanta, Mr. McRand was figuring out his next move. He was hoping it would never come to this, but in the meantime, he had to cover his own tracks. He knew he couldn't fully trust Ty because Ty was a man out of control. He formed a legion with the devil. He was asking himself was it worth it. At the time it all seemed like a good idea, to finally avenge his grandfather's death. He called it a day of atonement. Now Ty have left him holding the torch.

The flight touched down at the Atlanta Hartfield airport at precisely eight p.m. eastern standard time. McRand got off the plane. Reporters swamped him with microphones literally shoved down his throat, questions started flowing.

"Mr. McRand, what is your response to Maywell's claim of industrial espionage with their board member Ty Dannerman," one reporter asked.

"I have no comment at this time. All responses will by handled through Conquest legal department. Have a nice day ladies and gentleman, oh by the way Conquest thank you for your support," said Mr. McRand.

Mr. McRand picked up his luggage and was whisked away in a company limousine. The next morning at a press conference carried, live by CNN and other national networks, a company spokesman made the following statement.

"Mr. McRand vehemently denies any involvement in a so-called espionage plot with Maywell's former CEO, Mr. Ty Dannerman. Mr. McRand had no knowledge about Mr. Dannerman's espionage attempt to destroy Maywell. Mr. Dannerman acted alone and by himself concerning this matter and is trying to use Mr. McRand as an escape goat to protect his own interest.

"What about the contracts bids that Conquest out bided Maywell on?" a reporter shouted out.

"What about it. It was nothing- personal ladies and gentleman, just business. Conquest won those Conquest fair and square," said the spokesman.

"So what you are saying is that Mr. McRand had no prior knowledge of the contracts bid that Conquest won out on," said another reporter from the crowd.

"Precisely, said the spokesman.".

"What about the documents that Maywell officially have that links Mr. McRand with this espionage attempt?" a reporter asked.

"Documents can be forged. You can make a computer do anything you want nowadays," said the spokesman.

"Sir, "said someone from the audience.

But before he could finish, Conquest company spokesman cut him off dead in his tracks.

"That's all folks; there will be no further questions at this time. All these allegations are false. We will stop at nothing to prove Mr. McRand innocence, even if we have to go to court. This is just an attempt by Maywell to discredit Mr. McRand and Conquest. Everyone knows the bad blood these two companies have shared over the years due to strict competition to gain a greater percentage share of the market. Maywell is trying to get even, crying over spilled milk because they no longer hold a monopoly on the market, have a good day folks," said the Conquest spokesman.

Meanwhile Maywell implied that Mr. McRand had tampered with evidence that would directly link him with Mr. Dannerman. A Maywell spokesman said, "Maywell would stick to its claims that Mr. McRand was the mastermind behind the espionage attempt to avenge his grandfather's death." Mr. Aslong took it step further.

"Mr. McRand is trying to make us look like a bunch of cry babies, crying over sour grapes. That is not the case, Maywell handles adversity with the up most integrity, we don't cry over sour grapes. We lick our wounds and keep going. This is not a desperation attempt on our part to discredit anyone. An important part of our family is missing and that is our primary focus, to get her back safely."

He couldn't answer any questions concerning Nicole's case because of a gag order imposed by local authorities. This was a sensitive matter and he didn't want to jeopardize Nicole's safety. There wasn't even an award offered, not yet anyway.

Investigators searched Ty's mistress apartment and found incriminating evidence that Ty was indeed involved in the espionage attempt, which also link Mr. McRand. Local and federal authorities were both working on the case. They also found incriminating evidence that linked Ty to Ms. Flight's murder, his former mistress. Authorities questioned key witnesses in both cases and one of those witnesses was none other them Ms. Courtney Asmail. Prosecutors offered her a deal, a plea bargain and she sung like bluebird. She was pissed because Mr. McRand and Ty had doubled cross her.

Ms. Asmail had all the goods on the entire operation. When Mr. McRand heard this he ran for cover, out the country because surely this thing was known. Ms. Asmail had secretly recorded conversations between Mr. McRand and Ty.

She had incriminating evidence concerning Aaron's death and the spy network. Evidence that could put people involved away for a long time. Prosecutors felt that Ms. Asmail testimony alone was enough to convict both Mr. McRand and Ty. Her testimony also incriminated Mr. Cordova in which Pentagon official's subpoenaed records, which indicated, he abused the power of his office for personal gains. The Pentagon stripped Mr. Cordova of his power, ranking status in the military, and his pension he was to receive for retirement. His career was ruined. His attorneys accused the press of a modern day crucifixion concerning this propaganda. They also indicated that this was a personal vendetta because Mr. Cordova and the President were at odds concerning defense cuts. The President wanted to cut defense spending by closing military bases around the country while cutting back on nuclear weapons. Mr. Cordova wanted to increase defense spending by offering military personal pay raises while continuing to build nuclear weapons.

"Mr. Cordova had definitely stepped on a lot of toes and burned way too many bridges during his tenure here at the Pentagon. He has a hard time dealing with reality. He is too controversial," said one defense department official who didn't want to be identified.

CHAPTER
31

There was a nationwide search for Nicole. Local authorities and the FBI interviewed hundreds of people surrounding the case trying to find evidence that would bring them one step closer of finding Nicole alive. All leads were checked out thoroughly. There were some prank and bogus leads, but nothing could be taken for granted.

The President called Nicole's family to express his deepest regrets and vowed Nicole would be returned safely. Senator Gatewood and senator Thread were trying to pull strings to enhance the FBI efforts in trying to get information. Maywell finally offered a ransom, which was in the millions just to up the ante surrounding the case.

Nicole's mother heart couldn't take it. She just came to grips that Robert was still alive and now Nicole is missing. She wondered how much a person could take.

Authorities combed through abandoned buildings and fields, hoping to find clues of Nicole's whereabouts. An all points bulletin was put out on Ty because he was a flight risk. Authorities were stationed at the airports, bus terminals, and roadblocks were set-up hoping to catch him.

Ty arrived at the abandoned warehouse a little shaken because he didn't want it to come to this, but under the circumstances he had no choice. He was planning his own escape rout.

"Why did you do this Ty," said Nicole.

"Nicole what a stupid question, especially coming from a smart intelligent lady such as your self," said Ty.

"Ty you could have had it all," said Nicole.

"Look around you Nicole, I do have it all. I refuse to be denied. Those stiff-neck pompous SOB's at Maywell had to be taught a lesson. You don't mess with me and get away with it. That was a total national embarrassment ousting me as CEO and replacing me with the likes of you. A damn woman crying out loud, that was a definite no, no. I had the goods on them and they knew it, so that's why they kept me around. They knew I was a formidable enemy. Maywell was involved in some shady business dealing all initiated by me. If they had let me go I would have squealed like a pig and the U.S. Justice Department would have come down hard on their asses," said Ty.

"Ty you are a dysfunctional human being. You brought all this on yourself. Always shifting the blame, it's always someone else's fault as far as your concerned. It's all about money with you, isn't it?" said Nicole.

"Well that's the American dream Nicole. See, that is what I am talking about. A woman has no business running a corporation because they think with their emotions. Emotions do not make some company rich. It's about the almighty dollar Nicole, that's the bottom line. If a person can get their pocket greased in the process, so be it," said Ty.

"Funny you should mention emotions Ty. Cowards like yourself don't have emotions or any other pleasant characteristics that makes a decent human being Ty," said Nicole.

"Nicole I would shout the hell up if I was you. You are beginning to piss me off. And when I get pissed off there isn't no telling what I may do," said Ty.

"Ty I know quite well what you are capable of, murder. Just like you had Aaron killed, a decent family man. A man ten times better then you will ever be. So if you want to kill me, go right ahead. I rather die with integrity then live like a coward or in fear," said Nicole.

"Well you just might join Aaron if you keep running off at the mouth. You see that's another problem with women, they don't know when to shut the hell up, you all just constantly runoff at the mouth, some nagging heifers. Aaron had it coming. He was a thorn in my side so I didn't see him as decent, an irritation maybe, but not decent," said Ty.

"Aaron had more decency in his pinky finger than you have in your entire body Ty. You are a disgusting human being," said Nicole.

"Disgusting, isn't that a laugh? I'll show you how disgusting I am," said Ty.

Ty ordered the man out of the room. Nicole was ready for anything Ty had to dish out. She had nothing to fear but fear itself. She learned that from Robert, a man of courage. By dying, she felt that was a way to be reunited with Robert, spiritually so. When the man left the room, Ty grabbed Nicole and caressed her. He started kissing on her and touching her genitals as though she was a piece of meat. Ty begin to tear some of Nicole's clothes. Her body scent drove him crazy. He became a natural brute beast. She scratched Ty's face, which really made him angry. He slapped her and threw her against the wall. Her mouth was bloody. Nicole fought him off with every fiber of her being. No one had come close to her since Robert's death and she wasn't about to let it happen now, especially being raped. She would rather die then let a man like Ty touch her. She felt rape was just a violent act of rage by men to control women.

After he physically abused her and Nicole wouldn't give in to his advances, Ty decided it just wasn't worth it. He realized Nicole was a strong woman, unlike the women he is accustomed to fooling with. When Ty left the room, Nicole laid there on the floor curled up in a knot crying and badly shaken.

· · · · · · · · · ·

It was around noon, the kidnapper brought Nicole lunch, but she refused to eat. She was too upset to eat. She was prepared to die. The kidnapper had rough Nicole up a few times after she tried to escape several times unsuccessfully. He informed her that if she keeps this up that he would have to drug her. Nicole realized the kidnapper had a soft spot and that he was attracted to her, but he was taking orders from Ty. She remembered what her mother always used to say, "That you get more flies with honey than you do vinegar." Nicole started to have conversations with the man and eventually found favor with the gentleman. He would untie Nicole's hands and feet when Ty wasn't around. They would play cards and he gave Nicole pen and paper to write with, all which went against Ty's instructions. He would let Nicole listen to the radio. Nicole heard the news reports that the authorities were looking for her and that Maywell had put up a hefty ransom for her return.

Nicole pleaded with the kidnapper that she needed some fresh air after being lock up in a cage like an animal. After refusing several times the man finally agreed to take her for a short walk when Ty wasn't around only if she promises to behave herself. The man was getting a little edgy himself and felt that he needed some fresh air as well.

It was night, the beach was nearly vacant, and the reflection from the full moon made the ocean look like mingled glass. Nicole felt the vibratory breeze from the Atlantic Ocean. The waves were roaring like a mighty lion. The man and Nicole walked hand and hand, as lovers do. Nicole wore a black cap with her hair pinned up as a disguise. While walking along the beach, Nicole pulled out a hand written note she had written and dropped in the sand. The note read:

> *My name is Nicole Gershom and I desperately need your help. I've been kidnapped. Please contact the authorities ASAP. You will be rewarded handsomely upon my safe return.*
>
> *Sincerely,*
> *Nicole Gershom*

She signed the letter so authorities wouldn't think it was a prank in case they needed a handwritten expert to identify her signature. She knew the people at Maywell would know because she had a very distinguish signature. They walked along the beach about a quarter of a mile before they returned to the warehouse. Upon their return, Nicole got on both her knees and said a prayer, hoping that someone would find the note.

A federal judge ruled that Maywell would have to settle their dispute of industrial espionage through the courts. The U.S. Justice Department was investigating claims by Conquest that Maywell operated a monopoly. Judge, Alton Wiggins met with representatives on both sides and issued a gag order to cut down on the war of words. He sent a strong message to both sides by ordering them to stop fighting in the media. Plus, he didn't want to jeopardize or interfere the information authorities had collected surrounding the investigation of Nicole's kidnapping.

It had been a media circus; both parties were filing motions after motions. "This case could be tied up in courts for years," said industry analyst. Maywell wanted to try the case in criminal court while Conquest insisted on a civil case. Maywell executives really wanted to postpone the case because their main concern was finding Nicole. Maywell officials strongly felt Conquest was pushing the issue to revert attention away from the legal troubles of their CEO, Art McRand.

The media in its own rights went to court in order to allow the dispute made public. The media also wanted cameras in the courtroom, so they countered sued both companies. Industry analyst indicated that the case cannot be swept under the rug or solved behind close doors. This case would be monumental on how corporations handled their business affairs in the future.

The case had a political twist as the President indicated he would use the case as an example to bring harsh penalties against companies that engage in industrial espionage. The President made it his business for the U.S. Justice department to intervene due to the severity of the case. He also emphasizes that another crime has been committed and a young woman is missing. Nicole's return should be the primary focus. He issued a statement that both parties should put away their boxing gloves and return to their respective corners.

Maywell was in no hurry to try the case because that had documented proof how that the espionage plot damaged the way they do business. The plot also caused their stock prices to drop. Plus, they lost business due to the nature of them losing out on contract bids. The judge ruled to postpone the case until conclusive evidence is found concerning Nicole's kidnapping.

CHAPTER

33

Art McRand and his family were found dead execution style in Durbin, Ireland. Somehow, he managed to flee the country. He had a place in Ireland because of the country's no tax structure. Authorities knew he was a flight risk and ask him not to leave the country even though he wasn't formally charged with a crime. He informed authorities that he had to leave the U.S. from time to time because of Conquest business.

Even though no information was given concerning Mr. McRand murder case. There were speculations that Ty Dannerman had something to do with the killings. Authorities in Ireland found evidence that Mr. Dannerman and Mr. McRand were indeed in cahoots with one another. After all Mr. Dannerman was still at large. He was a flight risk. Authorities expected he would leave the country if he hasn't already left. Nicole's whereabouts played an important role in his scheme of things. Authorities were waiting on his next move.

Authorities got their first big break when a vacationer found Nicole's note on the beach and turned it over to the local authorities in Myrtle Beach. The walls were closing in on Mr. Dannerman. He called a friend on his cellular phone from his car about arranging for him to leave the country. Authorities had gotten a court order to wiretap Mr. Dannerman's phones. Authorities were quick to locate Mr. Dannerman

Lexus, which indicated he was in the Myrtle Beach area, the same area in which Nicole's note was found.

FBI agents quickly combed the area. Search dogs were bought in to search the area. Helicopters swarmed the area. Myrtle Beach look like Desert Storm without the scud missiles, but authorities bought in heavy weaponry for backup. Calls flooded the MBPD concerning men that look like Mr. Dannerman. Robert against authorities' better judgment was involved in the search. He was use to being in the heat of the battle. He was keeping his finger crossed, hoping they find Nicole alive.

Police had every reason to believe Nicole was still alive because a homeless man informed police that he saw a man and a woman that fit the description of Nicole walking on the beach several nights ago. The man explained to authorities that the man walking with woman guarded her very closely. He told authorities he was suspicious because it wasn't the usual loving couple he grew accustomed of seeing walking on the beach. Authorities had collected information from the Myrtle Beach courts that Mr. McRand owned property there in the area. Police dogs stormed the warehouse.

Authorities captured the kidnapper in a shoot-out. Authorities were in hot pursuit of Mr. Dannerman. They caught him several miles from the warehouse trying to get away. They pointed guns at him, told him to put his hands up. Mr. Dannerman slowly put his hands on the steering wheel and before authorities knew it, Mr. Dannerman pull out a magnum forty-four pistol, put the barrel of the gun in his mouth and pulled the trigger, He died instantly.

Authorities searched the warehouse and found Nicole tied together, as a lamb led to the slaughter. Nicole was unharmed. She was crying and shaking. Authorities untied her and told her she had a visitor; she was too distraught to answer, when Robert rushed through the door Nicole almost passed out. Robert grabbed and kissed her and held her ever so tight. This time it was for keeps.

"Robert somehow I knew you were still alive and would come back to me. I never gave up hope," said Nicole.

"Nicole! Nicole! wake-up honey. The movie "Walking in Vietnam", is over," shouted Robert.

The movie credits were still rolling.

Nicole jumped up as though she had seen a ghost. Robert held her tightly in his arms. She was shaking and trembling like a leaf on a tree, as tears were rolling down her cheeks.

"Nicole, sweetie it's okay, you are safe, let's get drunk, go to bed and make a baby," said Robert.